WILD ABOUT HARRY

BATEMAN

headline

Copyright © 2001 Colin Bateman

The right of Colin Bateman to be identified as the Author of
the Work has been asserted by him in accordance with the
Copyright, Designs and Patents Act 1988.

First published in Great Britain in 2001
by HarperCollins*Publishers*

First published in this paperback edition in 2013 by
HEADLINE PUBLISHING GROUP

1

Cataloguing in Publication Data is available from the British Library

ISBN 978 1 4722 0133 1

Typeset in Meridien by Palimpsest Book Production Limited,
Falkirk, Stirlingshire

Printed and bound by
CPI Group (UK) Ltd, Croydon CR0 4YY

Headline's policy is to use papers that are natural, renewable
and recyclable products and made from wood grown in sustainable
forests. The logging and manufacturing processes are expected
to conform to the environmental regulations of the
country of origin.

HEADLINE PUBLISHING GROUP
An Hachette UK Company
338 Euston Road
London NW1 3BH

www.headline.co.uk
www.hachette.co.uk

For Andrea and Matthew

Prologue
A Star is Born

Frankie Woods arrived in Ireland on vacation from LA in the hot summer of 1972.

Or to put it another way, Franklin Woudowski, having jumped bail after being caught with a glove compartment full of amphetamines, escaped to Ireland from Pittsburgh in the damp summer of 1972.

Frankie was just an ordinary American tourist. He did Cork, Galway and Dublin on the Monday and the Tuesday, leaving him Wednesday to squeeze in Belfast and the rest of the north, preferably before lunch.

Or to put it another way, Franklin bounced cheques in three cities south of the border and was bouncing his way around the north when the car he'd hired with his dodgy American Express card gave up the ghost just outside a picturesque little village on the shores of Belfast Lough.

Lacking the resources – for the moment – to get the vehicle fixed, Franklin lifted his army surplus bag and started walking. He wasn't army, but he was surplus.

He still had a little loose change left, and as it was close to lunch time, and he didn't believe anything was ever achieved on an empty stomach, except *starvation*, Franklin sauntered along the village's main street looking for a restaurant. All he could find was a pub serving the kind of wimpy curled-up sandwiches the Irish seemed to have patented, but it was slightly better than nothing. He stood at the bar, chomping, crumbing. 'Say, whaddya call this place anyhow?' he asked the barman.

'Pub.'

Franklin nodded. The elevator clearly didn't go all the way to the top. 'I mean, this village.'

'Holywood.'

'*Hollywood*? Like in the movies?'

'No, Holywood, as in the dump with nothing to do and nothing to see.' He pointed to a carved wooden sign hanging over the bar. It said, '*Holywood Fine Ales*' in olde worlde writing. 'There's an "L" of a difference,' the barman said.

Franklin laughed. He liked that. An *l* of a difference.

The barman's eyes remained fixed on the sign. 'I made it. I made it because I was bored. Bored, bored, bored. I was bored making it, and I was bored when I was finished. And I still am.'

Franklin wasn't really listening. Hollywood. *Holywood*. Not quite the real thing, but close enough. Funny. Quaint.

Was it a sign? Was it fate? In the years to come, Franklin decided it probably was. Certainly when you put it together with what happened next.

Normally, normally, he would have made his way to the city, any city, and set about finding a job. You see, he wasn't a bad man. He was caught with a few soft drugs, he was young, he wasn't doing any harm. And the dishonesty, the bounced cheques? It was just surviving. Given the chance to go straight, he'd take it. Maybe not straight; slightly curved might have been closer to the mark, but essentially he was a good guy.

But this time, he stayed in the pub. He enjoyed a few pints of Guinness, looking out over Belfast Lough. Then as darkness fell, and still with little notion as to where he was going to sleep or how he was going to pay for it, he found himself watching a small black and white television playing in the corner. The pub had been mostly empty during the day, but with the evening it started to fill up. He was soon chatting away with . . . well, *everyone*. He was like that. A talker, a charmer, an American in a country that still had fond memories of GIs during the war and for whom John Wayne was the greatest actor in the history of the stage (*the stage-coach, more like!* That got a big laugh). Soon they were buying him drinks. Wouldn't let him reach into his own empty pocket.

There was a local programme playing on the television. *Tea Time with Tommy.* A half-assed attempt at a variety show. 'Man – that really sucks,' Franklin roared. 'How do you watch this crap?' But he said it in such a way that they all laughed and agreed.

All except one guy, a thin, balding man in glasses who hugged his Guinness a little closer and said, 'I think a lot of hard work probably goes into it. I'm sure.'

'Sure, it does!' Franklin boomed. 'But if you don't get the basics right, then all that hard work might as well be pissin' in the wind.'

'Well, I'm sure they . . .'

Franklin counted off on his fingers. 'They got no script, they got no star, they got no *charisma*. Without charisma, you got shit. Sorry, brave effort, but you got shit.'

'You sound like you know something about TV.'

'Well, y'know.'

'Do you work in TV back there?'

Franklin shrugged. 'Well, y'know. I dabble. You wouldn't have heard . . .'

'No, really, I'm interested. I know a little myself.'

'You ever hear of Milton Berle?'

'The comedian? Of course I have. You work with him?'

'Well, kind of, he does some stuff for us.'

'Us?'

Franklin shrugged. 'Yeah. You probably wouldn't have heard of . . . you heard of NBC?'

'You work for NBC? For Milton Berle?'

Franklin took another sip of his drink. 'Well, I suppose, to be perfectly honest, he works for me. I produce Milt's show. It's good fun. I used to do Bob Hope's, but, well, that got boring.'

He could bullshit all night. What did they know? What harm could it do? He had actually worked in television. Six months for an NBC affiliate in Pittsburgh, selling local advertising for the commercial breaks in shows like Milton Berle's.

The guy with the glasses was staring at him intently. For the first time a little shiver of doubt ran through Franklin. What if the guy was a cop, what if those bounced cheques had caught up with him, what if the drugs charges had followed him to Ireland? He took another drink and concentrated on the TV.

'Excuse me, sir?'

Franklin turned slowly. He nodded. The man extended his hand. 'Michael Caldwell. I'm the managing director of Belfast Television. We . . . ahm . . . make that show. I don't suppose there's any possibility that we could hire you for a few weeks, just to advise us on our programming?'

'Well, I . . .'

'I realize it's very forward of me, and I'm sure we're very small fry compared with what you're used to, but we'd be prepared to pay you – as you would say, top dollar – for the benefit of your experience.'

Franklin Woudowski finished his pint, set it on the bar, glanced at the television, rubbed thoughtfully at his chin, then turned and extended his hand. 'Frankie Woods would be delighted to help,' he said, doing his best not to grin from ear to ear.

It was only for three weeks.

Five years later, Frankie Woods had an expansive house overlooking Holywood Golf Club and Belfast Lough. He was Director of Light Entertainment at Belfast Television. His girth was as ample as his bank account. Although they were indeed dark and deadly times for the population of that troubled province, the murder and the mayhem barely impinged on the televisual world of Frankie Woods. His role in life was to create a different, simpler, less painful existence, an alternative reality, a world in which trouble was a faulty autocue, a speechless child or a recalcitrant guest. His world was *Tea Time with Tommy*.

Despite all his best efforts, Frankie had never been able to get rid of the star of the show, the anchor that was weighing it down, Tommy Trainor.

Tommy was a throwback to the dance hall days. All singing, all dancing, all second-rate jokes. He was an institution, and should have been in one. He couldn't open his mouth without a joke coming out. He couldn't speak to anyone, even close friends, without dancing around them. He was pathologically unfunny, and yet, and yet, the show was a ratings triumph. In production meetings Frankie argued until he was blue in the face. Of course it was a ratings triumph, there were only the two BBC channels to compete against, and neither of them were likely to stoop to mere light entertainment at that time of night when the hard-working man was returning home wanting to catch up on the news of the day. It was a BBC rule that if there was death and despair in the air, it was also on the air. *Tea Time with Tommy* couldn't lose because nobody wanted to be *that* depressed every night. They could recruit a puppet rat to present *Tea Time with Tommy* and it would still be a ratings triumph.

But the owners didn't want to kill the goose that laid the golden eggs. So he was stuck with Tommy, all singing, all dancing, all . . . *heart condition*?

'I'm very sorry to hear that, Tommy.'

'Not as sorry as I am. I hardly had the heart to tell you. Boom boom.'

'But how is it going to affect . . .'

'Doctor wants me to cut down on my work.'

'Well, that's understandable.'

'Instead of the usual hundred and fifty per cent, from now on, it's strictly one hundred and forty-nine.' Tommy cackled.

Tommy was a laugh a month. The only concession he granted to his failing health was a slight restructuring of the show. The *Galloping Gourmet* was all the rage across the water, and Frankie reckoned something similar might work on *Tea Time with Tommy*, maybe a ten-minute segment which would give Tommy a chance to rest up. Bring someone new and fresh in, a protégé Frankie could build up, groom for stardom.

Three weeks later young Harry McKee walked

into the studios of Belfast Television expecting to change the world. He was a reporter for the *Belfast Telegraph*, but was known more for the mordantly witty television review column he wrote for it once a week. He hadn't been afraid to stick the knife into *Tea Time with Tommy*, even in this very week when he knew he was coming to Belfast Television for a job interview.

He had balls. He had principles. He had no idea the job was on *Tea Time with Tommy*. They had kept it deliberately vague. It was 'an exciting opportunity at the cutting edge of television'.

He sat in the production office, sixth guy they'd seen that morning. He flicked at a fine powder on his lapels. 'Marshmallows,' he said. 'My wife's an addict.' He spoke eloquently, but Frankie wasn't listening. He was sizing him up. Harry McKee was hardly what one would consider handsome, but he certainly wouldn't frighten people away, and when he smiled there was a little twinkle in his eyes that was quite endearing. He was young yet, but there was already a certain roguishness about him. He was big, but not beefy. He would probably run to flab in his later years, but now the slight puppyishness was rather appealing. And his voice: it had the kind of soft campness Frankie had come to associate with middle-class Belfast men; it was definitely a voice he could work at, perhaps play up the fruitiness a little; ladies loved that. Frankie was marking all of the candidates out of ten. The best of the rest had barely scraped past three. And he was the one with the stutter. Frankie's pen hovered over the little square box where he was to fill in the mark. What, seven? Frankie glanced up.

'I believe that television can reach an audience that newspapers no longer do,' Harry was saying, his voice rich with conviction, 'that it really can make a difference to our divided society, that if people think about their culture, embrace the things we share rather than highlight what keeps us apart, then perhaps we can move to a higher plane. Wasn't it Walt Whitman who said . . .'

'Harry – can you cook?'

The fact was, he could hardly butter toast.

Frankie did the hard sell anyway, persuading him at least to do a screen test instead of dashing out of the building, which was his initial reaction. Frankie even persuaded the crew to give Harry an ill-deserved round of applause after his floundering performance. He'd done his best, but it hadn't been good enough. Frankie didn't even bother watching the tapes. He thanked Harry for coming in and let him go back to his newspaper.

Then a few days later one of his production assistants called him in and said she'd something to show
him, and she played him Harry's tape and, good God,
but wasn't he just magic on screen? Frankie had
been there on the studio floor, shepherding Harry
through the moves and had sensed none of it. He'd
been clumsy and awkward and . . . but on tape, on
screen, there was a kind of humorous fluency to it.
With a little practice, why, they might actually have
something after all. Frankie glowed. His initial
instinct had been right. He picked up the phone and
called Harry.

Harry said no.

'Harry, c'mon. We love the tape. You're a natural.'

'No, I'm not.'

'Yes, you are. I've worked with some of the greats
in my time and I've never seen anyone with as much
raw . . .'

'Cut the crap.'

Frankie hadn't been spoken to like that in a while.
He spluttered on his cigar. 'Okay . . . okay, Harry,
have it your way. I think you show promise. I think
you could do great things on live television. But
you're right. Sure. Why rush it? All I'm talking about
is a little cookery. There's nothing to stop you continuing your career at the *Telegraph*. All I'm saying is
give me a couple of hours, twice a week.'

'I can't cook.'

'Doesn't matter. You'll learn.'

'I'm a news reporter.'

'And you always will be. Besides, there's always openings here for television reporters. The important thing is to get your foot in the door. You know that.'

There was a hesitation at the end of the line. *Got him*. Frankie hadn't spoken to the newsroom in years, but he knew fine well there would be no openings for Harry once his face became familiar as a television chef. They weren't going to send someone who fried eggs on a variety show to cover a bombing or a murder.

Still, it was only a little white lie.

'Harry, I know you're only married a year. I know you're expecting your first child.'

'How do you know that?'

'I hear these things. I also know what they pay at the *Telegraph*. It's a scandal. I don't know, maybe you have other income, but I'd say an extra two hundred would come in handy.'

'A week?'

'Nice try. A month. For ten minutes on screen. We can put you into every house in the land. You said it yourself, Harry, newspapers don't cut it any more. We'll give you the opportunity, what you do with it after that, well, that's up to you. Harry, I've been around, and I'll tell you this, live television, it's like flying an airplane, you start out small, you log as many hours as you can, then you move on to the bigger ones. Soon, pretty soon, you're in the jet set. Do you hear what I'm saying?'

Hook, line and sinker.

Three weeks later, Harry made his debut. One week after that there was a sackful of mail saying how wonderful he was, and what a comic touch he had. They had no way of knowing that little of it was intentional. That the eggs being dropped weren't in the script; that the pan fire wasn't pre-planned. That Frankie and the station's management were on the point of giving him the chop.

But popularity was popularity, and charisma was . . . charisma.

Sensing a shift in fortunes, Tommy Trainor went into overdrive. He huffed and he puffed and he squeezed more crap jokes into his already bulging script. He sweated and he worked and he mugged and on Harry's fourth appearance he finally . . . well, this is what happened.

Tommy was struggling for laughs. In the preceding weeks he'd given *everything*, but this evening his performance had been plodding and lifeless. 'Seriously now, I was looking at the wife the other day, and I thought to myself, why do women wear perfume and make-up? Then I remembered. Because they're ugly and they smell.' He looked up hopefully, but there was barely a titter. Frankie, up in the gallery, was determined to kick him into gear. That joke should have killed them. Tommy was falling back on one of his catchphrases in a desperate search for a laugh. 'The Milky Bars are on me!' he yelled and cackled, but even that old dependable fell flat.

As Tommy crossed the studio floor, Frankie breathed into his earpiece. 'C'mon, Tommy, give it a bit of *grrrrr.*'

Tommy turned to camera. 'And now for the man who's getting more mail than me – *grrrrr* – Harry McKee!'

Frankie rolled his eyes. The audience applauded with sudden and surprising enthusiasm. Harry smiled nervously as Tommy and his sparkly jacket stood beside him at the counter and surveyed the range of simple ingredients laid out before them.

'Well, Harry, my young friend, what's on the menu to . . .'

And with that Tommy clasped his chest, let out a low groan, and collapsed face down into the vegetables.

Frankie's mouth dropped open.

Camera One and Camera Two crisscrossed them-selves in confusion.

The audience began to laugh.

'Camera One – tight on Harry!'

Tommy rolled off the counter and crashed onto the floor.

Harry looked into Camera One and, without batting an eyelid, said: 'Something with a little less cholesterol than last week.'

The audience roared with laughter.

Tommy was dragged off stage and they laughed even louder.

Harry McKee took over the rest of the show, and he wasn't far off perfect.

Frankie, sitting up in the control-room gallery, barely registered that the man who had dominated his every waking moment since he'd joined Belfast Television had dropped dead on live television.

He was watching Harry reel off a stream of jokes.

He was listening to the audience in stitches.

When Frankie spoke, it was with awe in his voice.

'Ladies and gentlemen,' he said, 'a star is born.'

1

The sound of drumming reverberated around the house. Billy, in his room, was doing his best to keep the beat with Fatboy Slim, but his best wasn't quite good enough. Ruth, getting into her suit down the hall in her room, smiled, then turned her own music up. She hummed along. A knot in her stomach, but she hummed along. Billy would have described it as classical shit, but it wasn't really; it was an album of movie themes recorded by the London Symphony Orchestra. She suspected that they probably didn't include it on their CV, but she loved it, nevertheless. *Casablanca*. *Dr Zhivago*. She walked to the en suite in slow motion to the accompaniment of *Chariots of Fire*.

When she was ready, she stopped at Billy's

bedroom and poked her head around the door. He stopped drumming immediately and smiled hopefully up at her.

'Happy birthday, son,' Ruth said. She closed the door after her and turned for the stairs.

'Aren't you forgetting something?' Billy called after her.

'Later!' she shouted back, already halfway down the stairs. Before she reached the bottom the drumming had started again.

She smelled the kitchen before she entered it. The Cholesterol Kid was hard at work. She paused just before the open doorway, took a deep breath, then walked in. Harry was just shovelling a fried egg out of the pan, leaving a trail of fat between it and the plate on the worktop counter. Ruth ignored him and went to the cupboard for a bowl. As she poured her Special K, Harry turned his eyes to the ceiling.

'A musical talent is a great gift,' he said, 'and then there's DRUMMING.' A moment later the irrythmic pounding stopped. 'As if by magic,' Harry said, pleased with himself, though he'd really had nothing to do with it. Billy was late for school.

Ruth stood with her back against the counter, spooning the cereal carefully into her mouth. Didn't want to spill a drop on her best suit. Harry poured the last of the milk into his tea, then raised the empty cardboard carton, aimed and fired it across the room towards the waste bin. It bounced off the rim and landed on the floor. Harry shrugged and dug into his breakfast.

Billy came along the hall and into the kitchen, struggling into his school blazer. Harry, his mouth stuffed with food, said, 'You'll go deaf.'

Billy looked about him for a moment, his brow furrowed. 'What?' he said.

He poured a bowl of Frosties for himself and headed into the lounge. A moment later Ruth joined him. They crunched happily together while a Scottish woman discussed lingerie on breakfast TV. When the commercial break came Ruth set down her empty bowl and said, 'Billy – you know he's going to ask for custody.'

Billy turned his lovely dark eyes on his mother and nodded gravely.

Then they both started giggling.

As if.

Five minutes later Ruth sat in the car in the driveway, waiting for Harry to come out. Theirs was a big house on the way in to Donaghadee, a prosperous seaside town twenty miles from Belfast. The house had once belonged to a millionaire carpet manufacturer and had had every conceivable mod con installed. There was a swimming pool out back. It was overlooked by a separate block of spacious changing cubicles. There was a jetty out front where he must have tied up his cruiser or his yacht. Both, probably, and those of the jet-setting guests attending his regular parties. She sighed. That had been in the fifties. It was all different now, of course. The jetty was rusted and fractured. The pool was dry and filled with rubbish. There were boxes and boxes of things they would never use stored in the changing rooms. The detritus of a marriage. She sighed again. Once he was gone she'd get to grips with it, really smarten the place up. She drummed her fingers on the dash until Harry finally emerged, ushering Billy out and locking the front door.

'Do you want a lift?' Harry called after Billy as he hurried away down the drive. Billy put his hand to his ear and looked about him for a moment, before proceeding on down the drive. Ruth smirked, then wiped it off before Harry climbed into the car, already slightly out of breath.

As they emerged onto the road, Harry rolled down his window to ask Billy again about a lift, but before he could speak Billy had raised a finger to him and walked on. Harry thought for a moment about spitting something back, then shook his head and drove on.

Ruth went through the swing doors first.

As Harry followed, two elderly cleaners in blue aprons and clutching mops, spotted him.

'Hey, Harry! We love you!'

Harry stopped, a warm smile easing across his pale face. 'Why thank you, ladies, if I wasn't a married man . . .'

His eyes twinkled. They giggled like schoolgirls.

His eyes darted about, looking for Ruth, but she'd already entered the glass elevator. The doors were closing. She had her back to him. Harry tutted and headed for the stairs. As he disappeared from view he could clearly hear one of the cleaners saying, 'Bit of a fat shite, isn't he?'

The offices of JJ McMahon & Co, Solicitors, and Amanda Boyle, Solicitor, were housed in the same modern office block in the centre of the city, but they were light years apart in both attitude and decor. McMahon's was warm and musty, like an ageing university professor's. Boyle's was as cool and efficient as she was herself. She had a pudding-bowl haircut and a perpetually sour face. Ruth had been her client for several years. She had only ever seen her smile in triumph. Ruth sat across from her solicitor, and almost immediately found herself drifting.

'So, as we discussed last time, Ruth, almost an embarrassment of riches.' Ruth nodded vaguely. Ms Boyle, as she preferred to be known, patted the top copy of a pile of Sunday newspapers. It was upside down, but Ruth could see Harry's bloated drunken face staring out, the blonde with the wet T-shirt on his knee. Some showbiz party. The headline she knew by heart. *When Harry Wet Sally*. 'From what we have here,' Boyle was saying, 'I don't think there's any doubt we'll have him out on his ear and dossing in the nearest shop doorway, and nothing more than the mean son of a . . . Mrs McKee? Ruth?' Ruth was staring into nothingness. 'Ruth, please, stay with me on this, okay?'

Ruth nodded wearily. 'I just want it over.'

Two floors down, JJ McMahon was patting a similar pile of newspapers. 'Oh, Harry, *Harry*, where did it all go wrong?' Harry shrugged and took another sip of his whiskey. JJ had poured them both a generous shot on his arrival. They'd been friends for twenty years and knew each other backwards. So much of what he was saying was rhetorical. It was common knowledge to them both. But he still had to fight Harry's corner in court, even though his inclination was to wave the white flag and try to salvage something, even if it was only a clock radio. He shook his head and tutted. 'Drunkenness, unfaithfulness, it'll take the magistrate an hour to read the press clippings alone!'

Harry slumped down in his chair. 'Sure half of that's made up.'

'Aye, Harry, I know, but what about the other

half?' Harry shrugged again. 'What about . . . what about . . .' JJ began, flexing his fingers, clutching at straws. 'What about this time she threw the plate at you?'

'She was throwing it back.'

'Very difficult to prove. You had stitches?'

'We were *in* stitches, bloody plate wouldn't break.' He smiled briefly at the memory of it, as briefly as they had smiled then, a momentary respite in the permanent war.

'What about matters, ahm, conjugal?'

'We haven't conjugated in a long time.'

JJ sighed. He took another drink. He tutted. He lifted a sheet of paper with an official-looking seal on it. He tutted again. 'Harry, we go to the divorce court tomorrow. Unless you can come up with something by then, you'll be out on your ear without a leg to stand on.'

Harry nodded thoughtfully. He set his glass down. 'I'm going to have to kill her.'

JJ rolled his eyes. He lifted the bottle. 'Drink?' he said.

2

Tea Time with Harry, like many other variety shows of the time, was eventually put to death. But Harry himself was too valuable a commodity to lose. For a couple of years after that he hosted an afternoon chat show, then a panel game, before finally settling into *What's Cookin'?* the mid-morning show he had presented ever since. It mixed chat with cookery five mornings a week. The most popular segment of the show was called Dish of the Day. It featured a celebrity emerging from behind a set of venetian blinds to reveal his favourite recipe, then chatting about his life and career while helping Harry to prepare that very dish.

Of course, *real* celebrities were a bit short on the

ground in Belfast during the Troubles, and even with the coming of peace Frankie was still spending half his budget overpaying former soap stars and pop singers who hadn't had a hit in years to fly in to what was still regarded as a time bomb of a city. And it was, literally, *his* budget. Belfast Television had long ago farmed out *What's Cookin'?* to Frankie's own production company, Sunrise Television – they'd no choice, really, as Frankie and Harry had threatened to walk if they didn't. Frankie had boosted Harry's pay and even given him a director-ship and a share of the profits. Harry was quite happy to continue churning out *What's Cookin'?* five days a week, fifty weeks a year, as long as he could just roll in, do it, and enjoy the party afterwards. He wasn't really interested in running a company, or producing other programmes; he left all that to Frankie. There *were* other programmes; a nature documentary series, one on old Irish railways, one for teenagers, but none of them had made much of an impact and neither Belfast Television nor the BBC had asked for a second series of any of them. As they remarked locally, Frankie's bread and butter was his cookery programme.

So Harry was given a lot of leeway.

It didn't much matter if he occasionally smelled of drink. There wasn't smellovision, yet.

It didn't much matter if his skin was pale and blotchy, Lily in make-up could work wonders.

He still dropped eggs and burned things, but that was part of his charm.

Frankie was happy. Viewing figures were good. Advertising was good. The only thing that perplexed him and his team was the endless quest for celebrities.

Sometimes they scraped beneath the bottom of the barrel. Like today. Their guest was a flautist. Certainly *not* James Galway. Not even a teenage prodigy. They had to make do with one Brendan O'Maohoney, an elderly gentleman who played the clubs around Belfast and was best known for being able to play 'Annie's Song' while jamming a penny whistle up either nostril. Everyone was feeling too nauseous to even care what his favourite recipe was.

It wasn't even a case of being so bad it was good.

It was just bad.

Harry smirked through it.

The audience was almost asleep by the end of it. Frankie growled into his mike: 'Cue the fucking audience, half-wit,' and the stage manager shook himself into action and motioned the audience to applaud as Brendan removed the penny whistles from his nose.

Frankie watched the audience on his monitor as the camera panned across them. At least three quarters of them were of pensionable age. And the rest weren't that far from it. Harry's audience had always been made up of the elderly, the single mothers, the students and the chronically unemployable. As the years went by, peace broke out and the economy boomed, the audience had increasingly come to be dominated by the elderly and the infirm. There were just more of them now. Viewing figures hadn't dipped at all.

It wasn't *all* callipers and colostomy bags. At the end of each live show Harry did a little meet and greet, and it wasn't always out of the goodness of his heart. Quite often he forgot to remove his mike, and Frankie quite enjoyed listening in, laughing at how Harry dealt with some of the embarrassing requests, marvelling at how he managed always to sort the wheat from the fossilized chaff to zero in on the occasional attractive older woman.

There he was now, two old dears cosying up to him, cooing: 'We had to wait six weeks to get tickets.'

'Can we have an autograph?'

'And a kiss?'

Harry gave both, and posed for a photograph.

As the two happy old ladies toddled off, another

27

woman, a lot younger, perhaps in her mid-forties, with long blond hair, not bad-looking at all, in a certain light, came up to Harry.

'You must get used to that,' she said, smiling after the old ladies.

Harry, wiping at the lipstick on his cheek, shook his head. 'You *never* get used to that.' Frankie laughed. 'So,' Harry said, his voice soft but with a mischievous twist, 'were you looking for an autograph or a kiss?'

They moved off camera after that, and the mike was disconnected. But Frankie knew. Knew enough not to go barging into Harry's dressing room for half an hour. Or a couple of minutes anyway.

Lily, make-up queen on *What's Cookin'?* since its inception, and a good friend of Harry's, knew better as well. She didn't approve, but she was resigned to Harry and his philandering ways. The fact that her make-up room was next door to his dressing room and the walls were paper thin didn't help matters. Sordid was too short a word for what Harry got up to. Usually she timed leaving her room just as *she* was leaving Harry's, so that she could give them both a good *look*. She enjoyed seeing Harry's guilt, not that it lasted long. The women, well, it differed. To some it was like water off a duck's back. Others looked diminished, or disappointed at the experience or angry at the brush-off.

Quite often, after the show, Harry and some of the crew went for lunch at the Crown. Usually a liquid lunch. This day, there was only Lily. She had the afternoon off, and most of the rest of the crew were involved in shooting the latest of Frankie Woods's hare-brained schemes for a game show. So they sat at the bar, drinking, and after a while JJ joined them. By early afternoon they were all pretty drunk.

Harry had nipped out to get a copy of the *Belfast Telegraph* and was busy perusing the classifieds, his pint glass holding the paper in place. 'Now,' Harry asked, looking perplexed, 'what the friggin' hell does this mean – PPNPNGNS.'

'What?' JJ asked, blearily, leaning across the bar to study the page, the column and the ad Harry had his chubby finger pointed at. 'Oh, right, *apartments*. PP . . . what?'

'PPN . . . oh, fuck it.'

Lily leaned in from his other shoulder and studied the ad. She blew smoke down her nose and laughed. 'PPNPNGNS. Professional, Protestant, no pets, no gays, non-smoker.'

JJ laughed. 'Well, that's me out.'

29

Harry looked incredulous. 'How the hell do you work that out?'

Lily smiled. 'Once you're back on the single file, Harry, you'll get used to it.'

'Lily, you could take me in.'

'No, Harry.'

'Why not?'

'Because I value my freedom. And my sanity.'

Harry sat glumly, but only for a few moments. A smile slipped onto his face. He turned to JJ.

JJ, guessing what was coming, jumped up out of his seat and signalled to the barman for another round.

'JJ, c'mon.'

'No, Harry.'

'C'mon. You are my greatest friend. Apart from dental appointments and holidays, you've always been there for me.'

'No, Harry.'

'I swear to God I'd be no trouble.'

'Aye, Harry. And there's a pink pig.' He tried pointing to the ceiling, but he only managed to knock Harry's half-full pint over. Harry jumped back as the beer soaked through the newspaper. Lily giggled and slipped back away from the drips.

Harry folded the paper over as he tried to stem the flow of beer. The crotch of his trousers was already sopping. 'Fuck it,' he was saying, 'fuck it.'

'Sorry, Harry. Another on the way. Harry?'

But Harry's eyes were focused on the newspaper. There was a headline on the front that read QUEEN'S BIRTHDAY HONOURS and it was bugging him for some reason. He clicked his fingers, once, twice, three times.

'Harry . . .?'

'Hold on . . . hold . . . *shit*! Billy's birthday! Fuck it, JJ, why didn't you remind me?'

'Why didn't *I* . . .? Listen here, Harry . . .'

'Okay. Okay. Sorry. But it's his birthday, I have to get him something.' He sat fuming for several moments, then relaxed a little as JJ put his next pint down before him. The decision was made for him. 'I can't go anywhere with damp fuckin' pants, that's for sure. One more drink then I'm off.'

Harry stood, crushing the sopping paper into a ball, and handed it to the scowling barman. 'And don't be squeezing that into my fucking pint,' Harry said.

'I'll squeeze it down your fucking throat if you don't watch your language,' the barman shot back.

Harry was about to launch into his *don't you know who I am* routine, but JJ, who'd heard it once too often, pulled him back down onto his bar stool. 'Sit there,' he said, 'and shut up.'

Lily shook her head. Harry had a nose for trouble, an ear for bending and a mouth for cursing. She loved him as much as she loved any man, and she didn't love any man.

'So,' Harry said, after a few moments, looking from JJ to Lily and back, 'whaddya get the thirteen-year-old kid who has everything?'

3

Ruth had been planning Billy's surprise birthday barbecue for several weeks. *Surprise* and *planning* were the important words. She wasn't just trying to keep it secret from Billy, but from Harry as well. It wasn't like it was the invasion of Normandy or anything, but it was dicey enough.

First off, Billy's mates usually got the bus with him from their school in Bangor, six miles away, to their homes in Donaghadee. Now, she wasn't going to trust them to keep their mouths shut about a surprise barbecue, so she had to recruit their mothers to break the lazy habits of a lifetime to pick up their kids from school just for one day and drive them across to Donaghadee so that they could arrive at the house before Billy. She left it to them to come up with plausible excuses why they couldn't give Billy a lift as well. She thought she knew Billy well enough that he wouldn't be particularly miserable at the thought of a short bus ride home alone on his birthday. He was an easy-come, easy-go kind of a chap.

The mothers themselves would want to stay as well, and she was resigned to that. She wasn't particularly friendly with any of them. She had a nagging suspicion that they were only friendly towards her because Harry was such a celebrity. They were nice and chatty and always inviting her out, but every time Harry walked into the room, their attention always shifted to him. She was sure Harry had slept with at least one of them. The one who'd been calling round practically every day on the flimsiest excuses, and then abruptly had stopped.

She was paranoid, and she knew it.

But that was Harry's fault.

The important thing about the party was not to have him around. He would ruin it. The attention would be on him instead of Billy. He would start showing off. Performing. And even though he was more to be pitied than praised, he'd soon enough have a fawning crowd around him. Everyone loves a joker until they have to live with him.

Harry never came home before eight at night.

His work finished at lunch time, but he was never home before eight.

She'd long ago stopped asking where he went and what he did. It wasn't worth the hassle. He was drinking. He was screwing around. The newspapers told her all she needed to know.

So the trick was to hold the barbecue between four and seven and have it cleared up before he rolled home.

Claire, their daughter, called round early in the afternoon to help Ruth set the barbecue up on the wide balcony on the first floor of the house. The sun was out, strong and bright, the sea before them was calm, and the Copeland Islands, just a couple of miles away across the lough, seemed to shine. Claire and Ruth stood arm in arm looking at the islands for a few moments.

'Do you remember,' Ruth said, 'when you were younger and Daddy and I were fighting, we used to say we'd sail across to the islands and live there, that he couldn't get us there?'

Claire nodded sadly. 'Mummy, it was only a couple of times.'

Ruth nodded. 'For you, maybe.'

'Is there nothing . . .'

'No, love, it's finished.'

Claire nodded sagely for several moments. Then said gravely, 'I'll get the sausages.'

She skipped away. Ruth laughed after her. She was a good girl. They were both good kids. Despite everything. Claire had moved out of the house to go to Queens University in Belfast. She could easily have travelled up every day, but . . . well, Ruth understood. Claire got on a lot better with her father now that she didn't live with him. She was in her third year. Ruth and Harry, in one of their rare together moments, had tried to persuade her to study medicine. Her idea of compromise was to decide on a career in the theatre. Close, but not quite.

Ruth smiled. Claire couldn't stay for the barbecue, she'd an exam in the morning. But she stayed long enough to organize the kids when they arrived in a fleet of cars while Ruth got cocktails and sherries for the mothers. Then Billy's bus dropped him at the top of the road and Claire watched his progress up to the house with a pair of binoculars while Ruth shepherded everyone into Billy's bedroom.

Billy didn't notice a thing. The cars were parked out of sight around the back, and Ruth was watching *Oprah* when Billy wandered into the living room and slumped into the armchair beside her.

'Hi,' Ruth said.

'Hi.'

'What's up?'

'Nothing,' Billy said glumly. And after a moment, 'What's up with you?'

'Nothing, though Oprah's teaching America to read again.' He nodded. 'Billy?'

'Mmmm?'

'Go and put your school bag in your room.'

'In a minute.'

'Now.'

'In a minute.'

'Billy.'

'I'm watching this.'

'Billy, do what you're told.'

'Oh, for God . . .' He sighed, then got up and picked up his school bag. 'Great friggin' birthday this is.'

'Just do it, Billy, and stop complaining.'

She kept watching *Oprah*, but she could feel his thunderous eyes burning into her. She nearly lost it, but managed to hold on to her serious look until he'd reached the bottom of the stairs.

'Mum,' Billy called back.

'Mmmm?'

'Thanks for nothing.'

'Just do what you're told,' she snapped.

He thumped up the stairs with all the force he could muster. Ruth was giggling through her fingers. Billy tramped along the hall, opened his door and:

'SURPRISE!!!!!!!!!!!'

A moment later he was back at the top of the stairs, grinning, while Ruth stood at the bottom.

'Happy birthday, love,' she said.

'You cow!'

And then he was surrounded.

It was a great afternoon. Claire gave him a CD, and kissed him, much to his embarrassment. Billy stood behind the barbecue and cooked burgers for everyone. Worse, he made sure they ate them. Claire had to go after a while. Ruth stood with the other mothers and watched her drive away. She had a one-year-old Metro Harry had bought for her. He was good at buying things.

'Isn't she the great girl?' one of the mothers said.

'Yeah.'

'She's the dead spit of her father.'

'You mean she's fat and annoying.'

'No . . . Ruth, of course I don't. There's hardly a pick on her. She's just lovely.'

'I know. Sorry.'

Ruth turned back from the edge of the balcony and began organizing more drinks. They'd been asking her all afternoon what she was going to do after the divorce came through, whether she was going to keep the house, stay in Donaghadee, look for a job or maybe go back for some training, and the answer was yes to everything. She felt a little thrill. Tomorrow, D-day. Freedom. Sad, yes, but exciting. It would be like surgery, getting that knot untangled.

He had hurt her so many times.

He had destroyed her.

Ms Boyle was right. No mercy. In for the kill. You deserve it.

She was just handing around the tray of drinks when she heard the police siren. Distant at first, then getting closer.

Billy came up beside her, put his arm around her waist. 'They won't sell any ice cream going at that speed,' he said, grinning. He gave her a little squeeze. 'Thanks, Mum.'

She smiled, then immediately frowned as the police car pulled into their driveway. 'What the . . .?'

All of the mothers, and all of the kids, joined Ruth and Billy at the edge of the balcony as the police car, its siren still blasting away, travelled slowly up the drive before coming to a halt directly below them. The siren finally, thankfully, died. The driver's door opened and a policeman got out, looked first at the front door, then up at the balcony and the line of party guests. He raised his eyebrows at Ruth, then opened the rear door.

Harry tumbled out.

He landed in a heap on the gravel. A can of beer fell out beside him.

Ruth felt Billy stiffen beside her.

Harry slowly began to right himself. He forced himself shakily up onto his knees and then put one hand on the car to help push himself erect. He stood for a moment, studying the car, then reached around to his back pocket and produced his wallet. He opened it and began fumbling for money.

Ruth heard one of the women beside her whispering, 'He thinks it's a taxi.'

Harry finally produced a tenner and held it out for the policeman, who shook his head. 'It's okay, Harry – this one's on me.' Harry mumbled something and began to crush the money back into his wallet. The policeman patted him on the shoulder, then climbed back into the car and drove off.

Harry watched it for several moments, then turned towards the house. He was trying to put his wallet back into his pocket, but he couldn't quite get it to fit. His shirt was out and there was a dark stain on the front of his trousers. There appeared to be several buttons missing from his jacket. Ruth couldn't move. Nobody could. They were frozen with embarrassment, like they were watching an actor who'd forgotten his lines and was now stranded on a massive stage before the Queen Mother.

Finally Harry looked up to the balcony, at the mothers, and the kids, and Ruth, and Billy.

'What the fuck?' he said, his brow furrowed.

Nobody said anything. Harry scanned this surprise audience, and finally made out the outline of his son.

'Hey, Billy!'

Billy's face was white with anger.

Then Harry started to sing. 'I'd walk . . . a million . . . miles . . . for one of your . . . smiles . . . Biiiiiiillllly!'

Billy turned and stormed away.

Ruth glowered down at Harry, then went after Billy.

Harry looked perplexed. 'Billy!' he called. 'Hey, Billy! Where're you goin'?' He delved into his jacket pocket and produced an envelope. 'Hey! Billy! I've got you a fuckin' book token! D'ye hear me? Billy?'

4

It was difficult to imagine how Harry could actually make any more noise than he already was.

CRACK! CRASH! CRACK!

He hadn't exactly sobered up, but he wasn't as bad as he had been. He'd had a doze in his room and he hadn't had anything else to drink. But he was still quite drunk. There were no explanations given, and none were sought, on either side. He took it as a matter of course that Ruth and Billy would organize something like the barbecue behind his back, and they took it as given fact that he would roll in drunk and embarrass them all. It had always been like that, and would be for . . . one more night.

Now he was standing at the dishwasher, literally throwing plates into it.

CRACK! CRASH! CRASH!

Still humming that fucking *million miles for one of your smiles*.

Billy was sitting at the kitchen counter, seething, trying to concentrate on his Gameboy, but every CRACK! CRASH! and extended *Biiiilllllllly!* was driving him to distraction. Finally he turned and snapped.

'Would you ever shut up!'

Harry stopped, at least for a moment. 'Hey, Billy, what about it?'

'What about what?'

'You drum, I sing, we could play the clubs. Peters and Lee.'

'What the friggin' hell are you on about?'

'I'm serious. We could have a great wee act together.' Harry started singing again, throwing the dishes into the washer with even greater violence.

CRAAACK! CRASHHHH!

Billy quickly retreated to his bedroom. Ruth was already in hers, with the door locked. She had her music on again. Loud to drown out the cacophony of sound from below. She lay on her bed, then the noise was joined by Billy's drumming from down the hall. It felt to her that she had always existed in noise. It made her want to scream. But that would just make matters worse.

Later, when it had died down, she watched TV for a while. She sneaked out and kissed Billy goodnight, tucked him in, and they giggled about tomorrow's divorce. Then she went back to bed. She could still hear Harry moving about downstairs. She lay reading her book. It was a detective novel. The detective was a lesbian in pursuit of a gay man who'd murdered a transvestite in an argument over drugs. It wasn't doing much for her, but she'd started, so she would finish.

Then Harry was tapping on her door. His voice was slightly slurred. 'I was only having a bit of fun. I'm not drunk. I only had a couple.' There was nothing to say. She tried to keep her attention on the book. 'I'll bet you're following the words with your finger.'

Ruth removed her finger from the book.

'I always found that very endearing. Although picking your nose when you're stressed less so.'

Ruth removed her finger from her nose. She closed the book, then hugged her knees.

'Can we talk about tomorrow, Ruth?'

'It's all been said, Harry.'

There was a moment of silence, then he slapped the door with his hand, causing Ruth to jump. He wouldn't come in, wouldn't force his way in, he never had. But her heart was racing nevertheless. There was anger in his voice now. 'I know you think you're getting me out, but I have news for you' – there was a pause, and then a painful-sounding hiccup – 'and I'll tell it to you after the break.'

Harry hurried off down the hall. A few moments later she heard him being sick.

She sighed. She turned the bedside light off and snuggled down under the blankets.

One more night of this. One more. Ms Boyle had said those court orders took effect immediately. Harry should be spending his time packing instead of drinking. Come tomorrow she'd just tip all his crap out into the garden and change the locks. She smiled to herself. Then she'd start again. Her and Billy. They'd be fine.

She was just drifting off when there came another tap on the door.

'Ruth . . . honey . . . are you awake?' Harry whispered urgently. 'Darlin', are you awake?' His voice went up a couple of notches. 'Ruth, honey?'

'Whaaaat?' Ruth groaned. 'What is it?'

'Do you have any fags, love? I'm dying for a smoke.'

'No, I don't. Go to sleep.'

'I can't. I'm gasping. Not one?'

'I gave up, Harry. You know I gave up.'

'You must have one, snuck away for emergencies. Bottom of your drawer.'

She did actually, but she was bloody sure she wasn't giving it to him. 'Away out to the garage, get them yourself.' And then under her breath. 'Away and play with the fucking traffic.'

He slapped the door again. 'I heard that.'

Ruth smiled to herself. She snuggled down again.

Harry remained at the door. He began to blow: *wooooooooaaaah* like an Antarctic wind. 'I'm just going for a walk,' he said, his accent prim and English. 'I may be some time.'

Despite herself, Ruth let out a little laugh. She hoped he hadn't heard it. God. He could still make her laugh, the odd time. She'd loved him, once.

It was a little after one in the morning.

Harry meandered along to the garage. It was only a few hundred yards down the road. They'd fought against it being built there, along with the rest of their neighbours, a monstrous blight on such a beautiful coastal road, it was, but a bloody godsend at such an hour. He shivered against the cool breeze coming off the water. He only had on his light zip-up jacket.

The actual garage shop was closed, but there was

a serving hatch where a new young fella was sitting. Harry had been on quite good terms with the last kid to work the night shift, but they never lasted all that long. This one smiled keenly as he approached. Harry was willing to bet the smile wouldn't be quite so keen by about five.

'Forty Berkeley Menthol,' Harry said, and then immediately reconsidered. 'Better make it sixty.'

The kid turned from the hatch, while Harry got out his chequebook and a pen from his pocket and started to make out a cheque.

His arm was jostled and he said, 'Whoah, easy does it.' He smiled round at the group of kids who'd come up behind him. They were about eighteen or nineteen. Clean cut. There was a Mini revving behind them. Harry returned his attention to the cheque, only glancing up as the cigarettes were put down on the opposite side of the counter, behind the protective glass.

'Ah, sir, I'll be needing a cheque card with that.'

Harry signed the cheque and ripped it from the book. He put it onto the little turntable. His cigarettes were so tantalizingly close. He was dying for one.

'Cheque card, sir.'

Harry felt his jacket. Fuck it. He'd brought his chequebook, but his wallet with the card was in his other coat.

'Ah . . . look. It'll be fine. I . . .' He stepped back a little, and gave the kid his broadest smile. 'My face *is* my cheque card.'

The kid looked puzzled. 'I'm sorry?'

'My face *is* my cheque card.'

He was jostled by the teenagers behind again. One of them said, 'Come on, fat boy, hurry up.'

'Whoooah,' Harry responded, then sang under his breath, 'Arseholes to the left of me, arseholes to the right . . .' They pushed at him again, but he shrugged it off. 'Easy there, lads. Doin' some business here.'

'Sir, I'll just need a cheque card.'

'Look . . . it's me . . . Harry McKee . . . *What's Cookin'?*!'

The kid looked at him blankly.

Harry's eyes were feasting on the cigarettes. 'C'mon,' he pleaded, 'the cheque's fine. I'll pop around with the card in the morning.'

'I'm sorry, sir, I can't . . .'

'Hey, Harry?'

Harry turned, smiling already.

One of the teenagers headbutted him.

Harry staggered back, blood streaming from his nose.

Two of the others grabbed him by the shoulders and pulled him backwards. Another stuck out his foot and Harry tumbled over it, down onto the damp cement of the garage forecourt.

Once down, they couldn't resist it.

They began raining kicks down on Harry.

He groaned and tried to curl himself into a ball.

The kid was banging on the glass. 'Hey! Lads! Stop it!' His face crumpled in disgust as the feet continued to pound into the drunk. 'Fuck!'

They stopped, finally. They gathered about Harry, motionless now. They pointed, and together they chorused, 'What's Cookin', Harry?!'

Then laughed uproariously and fled back to their car.

All but one, who lingered for a moment, waiting for Harry to sense that all was safe. Slowly, slowly, Harry turned. His dropped his bloody hands from his face and was briefly dazzled by the forecourt lights. Then the thug brought his boot down with sickening glee on Harry's head.

The kid saw what was happening and forced himself to look away, but he heard the crack of it against the cement. Christ, he was nearly sick. He turned back to the window. The car was now leap-frogging away across the forecourt. Bloody joy-riders. The drunk was slowly pulling himself to his feet. His face was a mask of blood. He began to shuffle grotesquely towards the window, weaving left and right. Christ, he looked like Quasimodo.

'Jesus . . . sir . . . can I get you an ambulance?'

Harry steadied himself against the counter, and when he spoke bubbles of blood spat out of his mouth and against the glass. 'You can . . . get me . . . my cigarettes . . .'

Harry pressed a bloody finger to the window. The kid pressed a button on his side and the turntable brought the cigarettes around to Harry.

'Thanks,' he said. He picked them up one packet at a time, slipped them into his jacket pocket, then turned and began to make his way home slowly.

5

'WILL YOU STOP THAT FRIGGIN' RACKET!'

Harry's voice boomed through the house. Billy gave the drums a good hammering for a further few minutes, then pulled on his blazer and went downstairs. Ruth was already sitting watching breakfast TV. She was wearing her best suit again. She had several sheets of the Winnie the Pooh kitchen roll she'd purchased by mistake tucked into the collar of her blouse to prevent drips from her Special K. She had shoulder-length cinnamon hair, although the roots of it tended towards grey at the end of the month. There were crow's feet, but they were fledglings. She was really quite beautiful, she just needed someone to tell her so occasionally.

Ruth, eyes still on the maternity wear the Scottish woman was introducing, said, 'Did you hear him last night?'

'The elephant clog-dancing?'

'Aye.'

'The nicotine-deprived beagle?'

'That's the one.'

'We should be sympathetic, Mother.'

'That's right.'

'On this day when we're getting divorced.'

'Of course. Although I was thinking more in terms of a national holiday instead.'

They giggled.

Harry had managed to doze off again, but the slamming of the front door, and the thrust of the wheels against gravel outside, brought him up sharply. He was in his vest and pants; there was ash on his pillow, and a circular black stain. His face was swollen and encrusted with blood. His head was banging. His throat was dry. He was never drinking again. He swung his legs off the bed. He could smell . . . what could he smell? It was . . . it was . . . his brow furrowed, and the furrowing caused him to wince with pain. He hesitantly examined the small gash at the back of his head with his fingers. Jagged and sore. He went into the bathroom and tried to get a good look at it in the mirror, but it was a waste of time. What he needed was another smaller mirror to hold up behind him. He searched about for one, but there was nothing. Ruth kept all her girlie stuff in her own bathroom, and her door was perpetually locked.

Divorce.

Fuck it.

He wasn't even going. He wasn't contesting it. JJ would do his best and call him at the station. Harry had a show to do. He had eggs to scramble. Damn it, but he could smell . . . *marshmallows*?

He was running late.

He took a shower, keeping it cool out of regard for his injury and avoiding shampoo. He tidied himself up, looked a little more human. He took four Paracetamol to try and stop the throbbing in his head, then drove to work. He smoked five cigarettes on the way, but he still couldn't get the smell of marshmallows out of his nostrils.

A single man again.

Peace and quiet.

Nobody to moan at him.

She'd never understood the pressures he lived under. The constant scrutiny. The offers. He was a celebrity. Celebrities lived a different life. She could have enjoyed it with him. But no. She could have gone to the parties, shown a bit of interest, but, no, rather be at home with the kids. It wasn't like he was out and about every night of the week. Two or three, tops. It went with the job. It was a *social* job. Half their money came from personal appearances, from making the right contacts with advertisers, from companies who wanted him to endorse their products. Did she understand that? No, she bloody didn't. Harry laughed. Since he'd started appearing in the papers on a regular basis many of the endorsements had dropped away, but the invitations to parties had doubled. He wasn't that bad with women, really, but who could blame him the occasional indulgence when he was locked out of *her* bedroom at home.

Fuck her.

Harry groaned.

His entrance to Sunrise Television was barred by his nemesis, Ronnie McQuillan, the security guard from hell. Ronnie, decked out in a uniform that would have been considered too ostentatious for the dictator of a small African state, sauntered out of his Portakabin with arms raised, the gate barring Harry's entrance firmly in place behind him.

Harry had never quite worked out whether Ronnie was terminally stupid, just a frustrated action hero or a wanker who enjoyed pissing him off. Probably, it was all three.

Harry rested his elbow on his open window, with his ID card in his hand.

Ronnie took the card off him and examined it carefully. 'Mr . . . Magee, is it?'

'That's right, Ronnie.'

'And what's the purpose of your visit, Mr Magee?'

'I work here, Ronnie.'

'Uhuh. Just started, eh?'

'Sure, Ronnie, just last week. Twenty years ago.'

Ronnie nodded and handed back the plastic card. Harry shook his head and revved the engine.

'Well, just drive straight ahead there, Mr Magee, you'll find a parking space on the right.'

Ronnie turned and gave an elaborate hand signal to his assistant, Bernie, in a similar uniform with just a little less gold braid, and Bernie raised the gate.

'Thanks, Ronnie, you mad bastard,' Harry said as he drove through.

He parked in the space reserved for him – he fully expected that one day the plate marking it out as his would read *Harry Magee* – and then made his way down to make-up. There were a few curious glances on the way, but nothing was said.

Lily was reading *Cosmopolitan* when he entered. She didn't look up. Harry dropped into his usual chair and said, 'You're too old for that, Lily. You should have moved on to *Woman's Realm* by now.'

'You're never too old to learn,' she replied, then folded the page and set the magazine down. She got up, lit two cigarettes and held one out for Harry as she approached his chair. As he turned to accept it she saw his battered face for the first time.

'Good God, Harry, what happened?'

'Television critics. What do they know?'

The door opened and Frankie Woods came in. He saw the face immediately. 'Good God, Harry – what happened?'

'Television critics, what do they know?'

Lily looked at Harry. Frankie thrust a script into his lap. 'Can you make him presentable?'

'I haven't managed it yet.' She tutted, then bent to examine the damage. 'Ten minutes.'

'You have five.'

'Just go easy on the mushrooms,' Harry said.

'Mushrooms?' said Frankie.

'Mushrooms?' said Harry. 'I don't mean mushrooms. I mean marshmallows. Who's been eating marshmallows?'

'Marshmallows?' said Lily.

'Aye, marsh . . .' Harry began, then shook himself. 'What're we talking about marshmallows for, haven't we a show to do?'

'That's right, Harry,' said Frankie. He looked at Lily, rolled his eyes, then hurried from the make-up room. Damn Harry and his hangovers; he'd have to work extra hard today to keep him on track.

Luckily, luckily, their guests of the day were polished performers. Walter Adair and his lovely wife Tara. Walter was the Assembly member for South Belfast. He was young yet, only in his early thirties, but he was widely expected (not least by himself) to figure in the First Minister's autumn cabinet reshuffle. He was cool, charming, professional and charismatic. He made Frankie's skin crawl. His wife wasn't much better. Beautiful, in a tight-assed kind of a way, bright and as ready with a sound bite as her husband; but she was detached, or at least semi-detached. She could charm you into thinking you were her best friend, she would get your life story from you at the drop of a hatpin and you'd go away thinking that you'd got hers, but later you'd realize you'd got nothing but sound bites and platitudes.

Still.

Harry, looking slightly better, joined Frankie and together they waved across at Walter and Tara, standing in the doorway of the Green Room having their mikes fitted.

'Look at them,' Frankie said, 'like butter wouldn't melt . . .' He sighed. 'Still, they're cheap, and they give good television. A year from now they won't touch us with a fucking barge pole.'

'Do you smell marshmallows?' Harry asked, looking around him.

'*Concentrate*,' Frankie scolded, swiping Harry with his script. 'The key words here are family values, family values and . . . ahm . . . family values. Which is good, because I hear he's got families all over the fucking shop.'

Harry smiled stupidly. He stuck a finger in his ear and twirled it around. He wasn't quite hearing everything. It all sounded a little *muffled*. He heard *fugshop*. He delved. He swallowed, like he was on a plane. There, a little better.

Frankie nudged him. 'I know for a fact he's shagging that woman Hislop from the *Telegraph*. And you know that guy with the beard, does the farming programme? Walter's ploughing not such a lonely furrow with him.'

'He's . . .?'

'Yup, word on the street is he takes it both ways.' Frankie did a little Groucho move with his cigar. 'And I don't mean from the left and the right.'

'What fight?' said Harry.

'Not fight, *right*. God sake, Harry, *concentrate*. C'mon.' He smoothed down Harry's lapels. 'Okay. Let's keep it fluffy like your scrambled eggs, light like your pastry. Now smile. Okay?'

Harry smiled.

Frankie patted his shoulders. 'Okay. And try not to think about him up someone's ass.' He winked and began to walk towards the Green Room. 'Walter!' he cried. 'How are you?'

Harry followed a moment later, still sniffing for marshmallows.

6

They were all out there watching. The mad, the sad and the bad. The feckless, the thankless and the witless. They gathered in the activity rooms of old people's homes, of hospitals and prisons. The old, the cold and the bold fought over the seating arrangements as the intro to *What's Cookin'?* faded, as Harry bounded on stage, gathering a flying tea towel from one of the floor managers and smiling willingly to camera while the audience went crazy yelling, 'WHAT'S COOKIN', HARRY?'

'Good *morning* everyone, and welcome to the show!' Thousands were poised with notebooks and pencils to record the morning recipe, others would tape it, or probably tape the wrong channel, or over their husband's prized tape of Manchester United winning the European Cup. Harry's daughter Claire was watching it, hoping for a little buzz before she went for her exam. JJ in his office was watching it, pulling on his coat, ready to go to court to divorce Harry from his wife. And his wife Ruth was watching it, sitting in Ms Boyle's reception area waiting for her to come off the phone. Ms Boyle was two rooms away, but Ruth could clearly hear her biting someone's head off.

'Today – chickens. If free-range hens are oven ready, does that make battery hens Ever Ready?'

The audience laughed. Ruth knew there was a man standing in front of them holding a card with LAUGH written on it. She searched about for the remote control, but couldn't find it.

'They used to say go to work on an egg, but I prefer to go to work on my material . . .'

Ruth switched the television off. JJ was on the point of doing the same, but then decided to pour himself one last drink before heading the few hundred yards down the road to the courthouse. He needed it. There was something depressing about going into battle knowing with absolute certainty that you were going to be defeated.

Harry was now into his own recipe for the morning, reading it off the autocue. Frankie was sipping a cup of coffee, just double-checking the running order, when his assistant Christine nudged him and nodded at the monitor.

Harry was trying to read the words, but they kept going out of focus. 'That's half a pound . . . of . . . beef . . . fresh . . . tomatoes . . . ch . . .' Harry looked quickly down to the counter, checking the ingredients that were already laid out. 'Cheese . . . some . . . potatoes, yes, yes . . . and garlic . . .' He looked back to the autocue. 'Then we have . . . we have . . .'

'Shit,' Frankie said, 'the autocue's down.'

Christine shook her head. 'The autocue's fine. Harry's down.'

'Fuck.' Frankie bent over his microphone. 'Harry, are you okay?'

Harry, paused for a moment, then shook his head to one side, as if he was getting rid of water in his ear.

'Harry?'

'Yes, I'm fine.'

Frankie sighed. 'Will you stop answering me live on air?'

'Then stop asking me stupid bloody questions.' There was a ripple of laughter from the audience. Harry was mugging stupidly into the camera, like it was all a bit of a joke. 'And of course be sure to use skimmed milk, or you'll end up a fat bastard like me.'

There was an *oooooh* from the audience, and then some uncertain laughter.

Frankie seethed. Being clumsy and crap was one thing, they couldn't take the franchise away for that, but bad language on daytime TV, that was something else entirely. He drummed his fingers on the desk until Christine began counting Harry down to the commercial break.

'After the break, it's . . . Fish of the Day!'

'Dish!' Frankie cried into the mike.

'Dish of the Day!' Harry corrected in an instant.

When the theme tune had finished and the cameras were off him, Harry slumped down into a chair. He was sweating. His hair lay dank on his scalp. Lily hurried across and began to freshen him up.

'Sorry, I . . . sorry, I . . .' Harry was saying. His breathing was short, shallow and the pupils of his eyes were like pins. 'Can I have a gink . . . drink or something?'

Then Frankie was in his face. The temper had lessened somewhat. They still had to get to the end of the show. Then he'd let him have it. 'C'mon, Harry, a joke's a joke!'

'Sorry, sorry . . . I . . .' Lily handed him a drink

of water, and looked doubtfully from Harry to Frankie.

'Do you want someone to stand in, Harry?' Frankie asked.

'No – no, I'm just . . . flu.'

Christine was giving the countdown. The audience was being primed to erupt again.

'Are you sure, Harry?' Lily asked.

Harry nodded. 'I'm sure.'

Lily and Frankie hurried offstage just as the music began. Frankie made his way lugubriously back to the gallery. He was thinking maybe it was time to start breaking in a replacement for Harry, the way he'd done all those years ago with Harry himself. Someone fresh and charming and less likely to cock up on live television. Harry was getting on, certainly in television terms. He looked ten years older than he was. Someone who would do what he was told and not make an ass of himself doing it.

JJ fixed himself another drink. The court was only a few hundred yards away. He stood at the window sipping it and watched as the dreaded *Ms* Boyle and Ruth crossed the road and walked efficiently down towards the courthouse. *Ms*. Hah! She had the personality of a dead trout. *And I'm about to get beaten with one*. 'Oh, Harry!' JJ said and turned back to the screen.

The audience was going through its regular 'What's Cookin', Harry?' Mexican wave. JJ shook his head at the daftness of it. He loved Harry to bits, and all the more for the fact that he seemed oblivious to the fact that he made a complete ass of himself every morning.

'Welcome back, ladies and gentlemen – now it's time for . . . Dish of the Day!' Harry flicked out his tea towel like Zorro. Not that Zorro had ever flicked out a tea towel. He moved across to stand before a set of venetian blinds fronting a fake window and door. 'So let's see – who's behind the blinds!'

Harry opened the blinds with a flourish, and there stood Walter and Tara Adair, smiles in place, waving eagerly.

'The Assembly's finest – Walter Adair and his lovely wife Tara!'

The crowd, as directed, rose to their feet cheering.

Walter and Tara, with identical smiles, poked their heads around the door and waved. 'What's Cookin', Harry!' they cried.

'What's Cookin', Walter and Tara!' the audience roared back.

Frankie lit another cigar and rolled his eyes at Christine. She lit a cigarette herself. Then giggled and nodded at the monitor. Part of the fun of Dish of the Day was Harry putting tags on the guests with their names in big childish letters; the guests thought it was a joke, but it was to remind Harry who they were because they were usually so obscure. But now Harry had the Tara sticker on Walter, and was pressing the Walter sticker to Tara's breast. She let out a little *oooh!* and took a step backwards. Harry, impervious, threw his tea towel over his shoulder and smiled broadly to camera.

'Now then, Walter and Tara Adair, what's your . . . Dish of the Day?'

Walter gave an almost Nazi salute while he milked yet more applause. 'Well, Harry, it's something very close to my heart. To start with, an Ulster casserole . . .'

Spontaneous applause.

As Walter smiled and saluted again, Harry cut in with: 'Or an occupied six counties casserole, depending on your point of view.'

Walter's smile faltered. 'Y-yes . . .'

Tara, ever the supportive wife, stepped in immediately with a plummy: 'And to follow, choux pastry swans meandering in a pool of chocolate.'

'Mmmmm, scrummy!' cried Harry.

Frankie knew that there was no end to which minor celebrities and politicians – one and the same, really – would not go to get their faces on television. *What's Cookin'?* was a perfect example; here was a man destined for great things, a man who had been hailed as one of the finest young politicians of his generation, here he was wearing a white chef's hat, a red striped apron, and beating the hell out of a slab of stewing steak just so that somewhere further down the line some old dear would remember that nice young man who was on the box one day, and vote for him. Tara's role was to set up the stories or jokes so that her husband could deliver the punch line and look good.

She was already halfway through an anecdote about Belfast Zoo, a story that Frankie had first heard thirty years ago when he'd arrived accidentally in the Province, but now it was all dressed up as if it had happened to them just last week. Frankie was almost certain they'd told the same story when they were guests on the show the previous year. After a while, all the guests and stories just blended together, like one of Harry's dishes.

'. . . And as soon as the Mayor heard the zoo was going to buy a gondola for their artificial lake,' she was saying, 'he immediately announced that it made better financial sense . . .'

She stopped to allow her husband to finish the story.

'. . . To buy two gondolas in the hope that they might breed!'

Walter and Tara exploded. The audience, after some encouragement, joined in.

Harry, on the other hand, didn't react at all. Frankie wouldn't have noticed because he'd brought the shot close in on Walter and Tara's laughter, but Christine pointed Harry out on the monitor. He was concentrating intently on the onion he was chopping. *Really* concentrating, like there was nobody else there. The laughter faded, and then there was an awkward silence as Harry continued to prepare the onion. Walter looked at Tara, and they both looked at Harry. When Harry didn't say anything, Walter returned to beating his meat, and Tara lifted her wooden spoon and joined in too.

'Harry!' Frankie hissed into his microphone. 'Harry . . . !'

It was then that Walter and Tara saw drops of blood splashing down onto the cutting board from Harry's nose.

Harry himself, chopping steadily, didn't seem to notice it at first. Then he looked at it for several moments, trying to work out what it was. Finally he shook himself, pinched his dripping nose and laughed to camera. 'Little bit of extra flavour there.'

He lifted the chopping board and scraped the chopped onion, with its bloody sauce, into the saucepan sitting on top of the cooker. Tara and

Walter exchanged disturbed glances, then looked out towards the audience to see if anyone else had noticed.

They hadn't of course.

Harry began to read from the autocue. His voice was firm and confident, the words were clear. The awkward little nose bleed seemed to have cleared up as quickly as it had started. But dammit, despite the onions, despite the blood, he could *still* smell marshmallows. 'Now, in a world of divorce, scandal and corruption, yours is truly a golden marriage; fifteen years you've been an example to us all.'

Walter was immediately back to form. 'Oh Harry, we have our little tiffs . . .' He grinned at Tara, she grinned back. 'But the secret of our marriage is never go to bed on an argument, kiss and make up.'

Harry heard Frankie's relieved, jovial voice in his earpiece. 'I hope you're listening.'

Harry smiled, then continued nodding at Walter. 'Uhuh,' he said.

Tara placed a hand on her husband's shoulder. 'If more couples took the time to talk to each other, instead of running to the courts every time they had a tiff then . . .' She nodded at Walter, giving him his cue.

'I just think you have to work at a marriage, it's much too easy to just walk away these days. Marriage,

Harry, is like a casserole. The more you put into it, the longer it lasts.'

Even as the audience was responding with a spontaneous *aaaawwwwww*, Hany burst in with an exuberant, 'If only that were true!'

'Ah, but it is, Harry,' Walter scolded, and then turned his attention to the audience at home. If there'd been a soap box there he would have climbed upon it. 'And I'm not just referring to marriage here, Harry,' he began, 'but all of the problems that we as a society face in . . .'

Harry wasn't listening to any of it. He had a large misshapen carrot in his hand. He wagged it at Tara. 'Don't you think this looks like a really big penis?'

Tara's mouth dropped open.

Walter's polemic on society's ills trailed away into the void.

Up in the gallery Frankie said to everyone and no one: 'Did he just say *penis*?'

Across the country old people choked on their biscuits.

The audience in the studio was in a flap, but for Harry, contentedly slicing the carrot, nothing seemed amiss. 'So who would be doing the cooking at home then?' he asked.

Walter was gripping the worktop, desperately trying to retain his composure. His eyes were darting about, looking for reassurance, for relief. Tara was staring at the carrot.

'I . . . I . . . love to cook . . .' Walter began hesitantly, his eyes imploringly settled on the floor manager, but he was too stunned to offer any help. 'I'm out nearly every . . .'

Tara was clawing at his arm. 'So it's all down to me.' She was telling herself: *live television, live television, audience of thousands, live television, hang on in there . . .* 'Some nights I prepare a full . . .'

'Marshmallow, yes,' Harry cut in.

'Marshmallow?' said Tara.

'Frank? What'll we do?' Christine asked in the gallery.

Frankie whispered, 'Don't do this to me, Harry.'

Harry had his finger in his ear again. He shook his head. There *was* a fog in there. There was that smell again. He couldn't quite work out what was going on. Carrots. Onions. Who are these people? Tara . . . Walter . . . their name tags back to front. He laughed. Yes, yes – Walter, of course, Walter Adair, what had Frankie said, what was it . . . shit, cameras, TV, perform, *perform*!

Harry turned to the other saucepan on the cooker and lifted the lid. He waved away the steam. 'You just keep par-boiling these, but be sure you don't overcook them . . .' He pressed a fork into the saucepan of boiling potatoes and lifted one out, then examined it admiringly. 'Ah yes, nice firm young bodies. You'd be an authority on those now, Walter.'

'I'm sorry?'

'I mean, how you get away with it, I do not know. I only have to sneeze and it's all over the papers the next morning, and there's you out shaggin' every night of the week, and not a word about it!'

Harry plopped the potato back into the pot.

Walter could feel Tara's eyes burning into him. 'I'm sure . . . I don't know what you . . . Is this some sort of a . . .'

Harry slammed down the saucepan lid, making everyone jump. 'I'm only telling you what I hear on the street!' he cried. His eyes were wide now, the words speeding out. 'The Hislop woman with the beard, from the left and the right! Is that clear enough for you!?'

Frankie couldn't move. Really couldn't move. Not even his tongue.

'Now, I've nothing against men and men,' Harry continued. 'I mean my best friend . . .' and he winked at the screen. JJ dropped his third drink to his office floor. 'He's well into all that . . .'

'Don't, Harry. Don't, Harry,' JJ urged the television. 'For fuck's sake, Harry, don't . . .'

'But he's not married,' Harry said, 'and you two are.'

JJ breathed a sigh of relief as Harry's attention shifted back to his guests. What the hell was he playing at? Was he completely and totally drunk? All JJ could pray for was that the magistrate wasn't watching. *The magistrate!* Christ, he was ten minutes late already.

JJ sprinted for the door, cursing, cursing, cursing Harry McKee.

But there was no such easy exit for the Adairs.

'Golden marriage, my arse!' Harry boomed. 'How do you keep the whole show on the road, eh? What's the secret, Tara? Do you kick with both feet as well?'

Tara, her face a mask of fury, pulled her chef's hat off and threw it down on the counter. Live television? Fuck it, she didn't have to take this. She slapped Harry hard. He scarcely batted an eyelid. Then she ripped the microphone from her chest and strode away across the studio.

Walter stood, finger raised and pointing at Harry, but quite unable to say anything. He tried once, twice, three times, then gave up and ran after his wife.

Harry nodded after him for a moment, then turned to camera. 'Okay, once you have your beef ready, you need just a pinch of garlic. Not too much now, never know who you might have to kiss later . . .'

He leaned over the casserole dish and began to mix the ingredients together, while the audience sat in stunned disbelief.

Nobody knew what to do. There was no direction from the gallery. They could hear Walter wailing into his microphone somewhere backstage. 'Tara! Please! A couple of women, but no men! No men!' And then a hard slap echoed across the studio and tens of thousands of homes across the country.

Frankie, recovering his motor skills at last, almost hurled himself at his microphone. 'Get that fucking mike off, Walter!' he bellowed, then turned his attention to Harry, pounding ingredients on a dozen monitors before him. 'You're finished, Harry! Do you hear me! I've had enough of your fuck-ups!'

All Harry was trying to do was to finish making the meal, that was what he did, it was his life, make the meal, make the meal, *make the meal*! And for all his efforts what did he get? Some arsehole cursing in his ear. What did people know? Those nice people sitting at home expecting him to cook a nice meal. They didn't know there was some arse spitting in his ear hole. Frankie was still in full flow. *Right* Right, thought Harry, I'll bloody show him.

Harry deftly removed his earpiece and tucked it

into the microphone clip on his chest. Instantly Frankie's venom began to reverberate around the studio, and around the country.

'They'll sue us for fucking millions!' Frankie yelled. 'You'll never work in television again! Do you hear me, you fucking asshole!' He thumped the control panel before him. 'Fuck! Fuck! Fuck! You're nothing but a fucking waster! Fucking talentless son of a . . .'

It was Christine's doe eyes and hanging jaw and her shaking finger pointing at the microphone before him that finally brought Frankie to the sudden realization that he had been broadcasting live to the nation.

There was a moment of absolute horror, when his heart stopped and his stomach fell into his shoes. He let out a little wounded cry, then buried his head in his hands and began to sob.

Christine was on the point of saying a final, exasperated, 'Roll titles,' but Harry beat her to it.

And then returned to his fucking mixing.

Frankie wailed. It was over, all over, they were ruined, the show, the franchise, the company.

Fuck!

Down below, the floor manager encouraged the stunned audience into meagre applause while the *What's Cookin'?* theme rang out.

Once the titles were up the crew stood looking

at Harry, unsure what to do. The production assistants stood with their files and their walkie-talkies, and none of them would approach while Harry mixed and mixed and mixed.

Finally it was Lily who hurried across to him and eased the wooden spoon out of his grasp and pushed him gently down onto a stool.

'Harry . . .' She put one of her hands on his, and he looked dreamily down at it, then jerked suddenly and said, 'Christ, is that the time! I have to get to court!'

He jumped up, staggered slightly, then hurried away across the studio floor.

'Harry!' Lily called after him. 'You have to see a doctor!' But he was gone.

7

It wasn't going any better at Belfast Magistrates' Court. JJ sat slumped in his chair, a beaten man. Across the aisle, Ms Boyle positively glowed. Ruth herself sat pale and straight, tense, expectant and even . . . what was it . . . *guilty*? She shook herself. *Come on, Ruth, this is what you've been fighting for. Enjoy it!* She glanced about the high-ceilinged courtroom, at the clerk checking his books, at JJ sitting with his hand under his chin, his eyes fluttering like he was going to fall asleep, at Ms Boyle with her pursed lips and glowing eyes, and finally at the magistrate. Her trump card, as Ms Boyle had described her. She'd sprung that one on JJ when they'd arrived. JJ had been expecting Basil Farnham to be presiding, and he knew for a fact that Basil had been stung for so much alimony by his own ex-wife that he was having difficulty making ends meet. Now that was *bound* to be in their favour. But he'd walked into court that morning to find Olivia Maguire up there, or Saint Olivia, as she was known on the court circuit. There was that much high moral fibre to her, she was like a box of celestial Special K. She was the Mother Teresa of the divorce court, and only slightly better-looking. She didn't grant divorces easily, but when she took against someone, she *really* took against them. Ruth just managed to suppress a grin as Saint Olivia's tutting, tutting, tutting echoed around the court. She was barely halfway through the reports before her. She tutted again at a sudden clattering from the rear of the court. Ruth turned just in time to see the forbiddingly large doors crash open. Then Harry was standing there.

JJ rolled his eyes as Harry shuffled down the aisle under Saint Olivia's withering gaze. There was something odd about his progress towards the front of the court; it was somewhere between a shuffle and a slope, with a hint of crab thrown in. *Great, bloody great,* Harry's hair was all over the place, his shirt was sticking out, there was blood on the collar, he was out of breath, pale, sweating, bloated. As he slipped in beside him, JJ hissed, 'Great, the rat joins the sinking ship.'

'*Rat?*' Harry jerked back, his eyes darting about, looking for a rodent.

'Right, Harry,' JJ whispered, 'fucking right.'

Ruth refused to look across. Couldn't.

'Mr McMahon?' The magistrate was peering down from the bench, her face frozen, her voice, cold, emotionless. JJ stood and nodded. 'This does not make for very happy reading.' JJ nodded. 'Affairs, drunkenness, disturbing the peace . . .' She glanced across at Ms Boyle. 'I take it there is absolutely no chance of a reconciliation?' Ms Boyle raised her eyebrows. It was enough. 'No, I suppose not,' Saint Olivia continued. She looked down at Harry over the top of her austere glasses. 'And you seem such a nice man on television.'

If Harry heard, he gave no indication. He could smell the marshmallows again, and now there was the sound of music. Not *The Sound of Music*. No! He giggled. He looked around, but couldn't pin down the source. Then it was fading . . . no, *draining* away, caught up in the rushing sound in his ears. Like going down a water chute to the sea. Like at Disneyland. He had been there once, when the kids were younger. What a brilliant time. And then he thought, is there a water chute at Disneyland, or was that somewhere else? Ruth would know. He began to get up out of his seat to go and ask her, she was sitting there just across the room. What were they doing, waiting for a plane? But why were they sitting apart? Oh, yes. The smoking. He was in the smoking section. Still, he'd just pop across and ask . . . but JJ put a firm hand on his arm, pinning him down. Okay. Okay, later. At home. He was bored here. He wished the case was over. He didn't like courtrooms. This was how he spent his life, listening to trials and then reporting them for the paper. He'd have to file his copy by one o'clock at the latest. He closed his eyes and tried to remember what programme he was supposed to be reviewing that night. Some new sit-com from the BBC, wasn't it? He was playing football in the park. His ninth birthday. Jumpers for nets. He scored. He was so happy. He giggled. He opened his eyes. He felt people were looking at him, so he hid his face. He tilted his head back and stared at the ceiling. There was a frieze. Ancient warriors. Spears and shields and what was that film he'd so enjoyed . . . *Jason and the Argonauts.* With the skeletons fighting.

JJ did his best to ignore Harry as he jittered beside him. He stood to explain, to plead, to apologize, always mindful that the most important thing was to prevent Harry himself from speaking. *That* would be bombing the sinking ship. 'He has the hectic work schedule one associates with a man at the top of his profession,' JJ declared to the Saint, 'coupled with the fact that he is constantly in the public eye . . . Inevitably there have been problems, but it is my client's fervent wish . . .'

Harry was looking across the aisle at the stout woman with the pudden' bowl hair cut and the lizard's tail snaking out from beneath her skirt. Reptiles in the courtroom! The scalies of justice! Harry giggled.

Boyle was on her feet. Hammering home the final nail in the coffin. '. . . That my client's ritual humiliation at the hands of this Jekyll and Hyde character be put to an end, with a significant indication on your worship's part vis-à-vis the division of property as to where the blame in this matter lies . . .'

The Magnificent Seven, The Wild Bunch, The Outlaw Josey Wales, High Noon, The Searchers, Dances with Wolves, Rio Bravo . . .

'Much as my client would desire it, your worship,' JJ said forlornly, 'he holds out little hope.'

Dopey, Bashful, Grumpy, Sleepy, sleepy, sleepy . . .

The magistrate nodded sagely, then paused, purely for dramatic effect, because *everyone* knew the outcome, even people who weren't interested and hadn't been born or who lived in the shanty towns of Rio de Janeiro. 'Very well, then,' she said finally, 'I have no alternative but to grant the . . .'

There was an almighty clatter as Harry, tilting his chair back, finally lost his balance and crashed to the floor.

The magistrate peered frostily over her glasses as Harry lay blinking for several moments. *Marshmallows.* Nice and fresh and warm, like a sweetie shop on a summer's day. He closed his eyes.

Saint Olivia banged her gavel. 'Mr McKee! This is not the place for amateur dramatics!'

JJ, standing exasperated, hands on hips, hissed, 'Harry – this isn't the way to do it.'

Ruth seethed. The bastard was always determined to put on the show, to be the big fella, the centre of attention. Well, he wasn't bloody well going to win this one. He was gone. He was out on his ear. He was . . .

A dribble of blood.

It rolled out of his nose, skirted his mouth and dripped onto the floor.

That's what got them moving.

In the briefest moment he went from fat figure of fun to an emergency case surrounded by concern. JJ, the clerk, a security guard, several solicitors preparing for the next case, all pressed around him, trying to bring him round. The clerk turned suddenly from Harry and rushed back to the bench. He whispered something in the magistrate's ear. Saint Olivia took one further look at the scene before her, then looked across at Ms Boyle and sadly shook her head.

Ruth looked at her solicitor in disbelief, then stood abruptly and yelled at the bench. 'You can't do this! Sign the bloody thing! Stamp it! Whatever the hell you do!' Her voice was breaking. 'I want my divorce!'

Saint Olivia was having none of it. 'Mrs McKee!' she cried. *'Settle down.* Ms Boyle? You know the law . . . Mr McKee is obviously . . . *indisposed.* I'm afraid you'll have to remain Mrs McKee until we can establish exactly how much of the proceedings your husband understood.'

'But he's a fucking chancer! You can't fall for this!'

Ms Boyle tugged at her arm as the magistrate hammered away with her gavel, but Ruth wouldn't be calmed. She had come so close. She'd been over the final hurdle and heading for the post, only to be struck down by lightning. She couldn't believe it. She *wouldn't* believe it. She continued to berate the magistrate even after the Saint had retreated to her private quarters, and was still complaining loudly to anyone and everyone as the ambulance arrived and the paramedics began to examine Harry where he lay on the floor.

Ruth finally dashed from the courtroom. She held

herself together until she reached the ladies. Once she'd bolted herself safely into a cubicle she collapsed down onto the toilet and sobbed her eyes out.

She emerged, immaculate, five minutes later. Ms Boyle was nowhere to be seen, but JJ, in his stained mac and baggy, tweedy trousers, was standing in the corridor waiting for her. He was trying his best to look sympathetic.

She was having none of it. 'This is the best yet, JJ,' Ruth growled as she passed him at speed.

He followed after her. 'Ruth, c'mon, I swear to God.'

'Aye, JJ.'

'I was going to give you a lift to the hospital.'

Ruth stopped abruptly. She looked him straight in the eye. He stared back, but only managed to last a few seconds before looking away. 'I'll make my own way,' Ruth said sharply and walked on. This time he didn't try to follow.

8

The downfall of Walter Adair was little short of spec-
tacular. *What's Cookin'?* was only the start of it. It
was merely the cork in the bottle. Once removed,
the stories and the scandal flowed like cheap wine.
The tabloids had a field day. The broadsheets,
normally one step removed, had a bloody ploughing
championship. So many people wanted to rat Walter
out that the *Belfast Telegraph* set up a special Walter
Line. Women, men, black, white, Protestant, Catholic
and even an agnostic all lined up to glory in their
shame. Mercifully, and much against fashion, there
were no children involved in the sexual shenanigans
– although they did tape one after-hours call from
a barking dog who seemed to have quite a serious

complaint. Cassette after cassette was filled with sordid, salacious and frankly embarrassing tales of fumbled sex and dazzling seduction. Walter, who had once been tipped to be a future First Minister of the Province, couldn't even get his election agent to pick up his phone.

Walter and Tara were holed up in their ten-bedroomed bungalow outside Hillsborough. The press laid siege. Their letterbox was forced open and stale men in stained coats shouted abuse in the form of questions along his hall and up his stairs and under the locked door of his study where he drank and cried and wailed and swore, while in the kitchen below Tara managed to cook and clean and pack and smash and yell all at the same time, although taking care to keep the noise down so that the men with their spittle mouths pressed against her door wouldn't be able to suck up more fodder with their poisonous little rags.

They were a team. They were one. She *was* Walter, and had been for ten years. When he farted, she said excuse me. When she had her period, Walter got cramps. When they died, it would be together, they would have a coffin built for two, and they'd laughed about how all their two-faced, hypocritical friends would suffer heart attacks trying to carry it to the church.

But now who was two-faced and hypocritical?
THAT BASTARD UPSTAIRS.

How could he? And not just with women. With *men*. After all his campaigning. All those nights when he was supposed to be working. While she kept the home fires burning. Or at least had a woman who came in and kept them burning.

THE BASTARD!

She boiled.

Simon Gray, their solicitor, arrived mid-morning. Good old Simon. Her friend. Her chum. How many parties, how many dinners? And there he was sloping along the hall and up the stairs without even a word for her, then locking himself in with Walter while they cooked up an appeasing statement for the press.

'DON'T CONSULT ME, YOU BASTARDS!' she yelled very quietly into the fist she'd put into her mouth to stop herself from crying.

She removed a moderately expensive bottle of wine from the cellar and had half of it down her in a matter of minutes. She covered the other half with a layer of Stretch'n'Seal so that she could use it later for that sauce she'd been talking to . . . What the hell was she thinking? Dinner party! There would be no more dinner parties! Not in this house! Not with that monster! She ripped off the Stretch'n'Seal and raised the bottle to her mouth. At that moment there was a flash from the window and Tara looked up to see a photographer grinning at her, happy that he'd captured that evening's front-page photograph of a wronged woman driven to drink. What he'd actually captured was eight stitches and a broken camera as Tara's bottle smashed through the window, spraying him with glass and knocking him off the ledge onto the immaculately laid cobbles below. (At £1.50 per cobble, they believed they had quite a bargain, and the blood *would* wash off. NOT THAT SHE'D BE THERE!)

In the early evening, with the glare of the camera lights spoiling the delicate pastel shadings of the lounge and hallway, Simon Gray hesitantly opened the front door of the Adair residence and stepped outside. He pulled the door onto the snib behind him. He was used to standing up in court, but this was something different. It was the lion's den, the eye of the storm, the . . .

'Where is he?' someone shouted.

'Send the bugger out!' yelled someone else.

A dozen microphones were thrust into his face. A series of flashes temporarily blinded him. He fumbled for the statement he and Walter had concocted. He lost his footing and stumbled back against the door. The door opened just enough for the reporters to glimpse Tara and Walter at each other's throats at the bottom of the hall. Simon quickly pulled the door closed again, but not before he, and therefore they, had heard the unmistakable sound of glass breaking. It surprised Simon. He didn't think there was any glass left to break.

Simon would have been there all night if he'd been waiting for a respectful silence to fall, so he cleared his throat and without warning plunged into the statement. 'Walter Adair wishes to assure his constituents that the sordid allegations aired on this morning's edition of *What's Cookin'?* are entirely without foundation' – he faltered as something large and expensive shattered against the inside of the door behind him – 'and will be the subject of legal action. Mr and Mrs Adair remain' – there came another almighty crash – 'devoted to each other and united in their desire to put this unfortunate experience behind them and to continue to serve the marvellous people of Belfast. Their phone has not stopped ringing with all the messages of support.' Simon paused for breath, then held up his hand as a wave of questions engulfed him. 'No . . . *no*! They will not be answering questions, although they have agreed to a brief photocall.'

Simon turned and tapped the door lightly. There was a moment of mild panic as it remained steadfastly closed, then finally there was movement, followed by an explosion of light as the cameras registered the arrival of Walter Adair MP and his lovely wife Tara, he in a sober grey suit and she in the challenging red two-piece she'd bought in Brown Thomas, their familiar smiles in place, holding hands, forcing warmth from their bodies, their eyes urging the world to love them.

But the world wasn't in the mood for love.

It was in the mood for blood.

The world did not require a placid photo session. They hadn't just become engaged. This was a man of morals who'd been boning half of Belfast, including men with beards. Here was a paragon of virtue who was a parallelogram of lust. They screamed their questions.

'Are you bisexual?'

'Did you make love in the First Minister's office?'

'How many were pregnant?'

'Do you prefer boys or girls?'

'Are you resigning your seat?'

'Has the First Minister called?'

'Do you fancy him as well?'

'Are you sticking with him, Tara?'

'Do you turn a blind eye?'

'Resign, you fuckin' fruit!' This last was from a passing taxi driver, but it was the straw poll that broke the camel's back. Tara backed away through the door, pulling Walter with her. His hand was bleeding from where her nails had dug into him. Simon followed them back inside and slammed the door shut. His feet crunched over shards of shattered crockery. Tara was already climbing the stairs. Walter stood at the bottom looking up. 'Tara, please!' he called, his voice despairingly weak.

But there was only a slamming door and an echoing sob that seemed to come up from her feet.

When Walter turned towards him, Simon could see that there were tears in his eyes. 'I've lost her,' he said.

Simon shrugged sympathetically. He tried desperately to think of something reassuring to say, but nothing would come. Instead he scurried into the kitchen and got Walter a drink. He was still standing at the bottom of the stairs when Simon brought it back. There were *noises* coming from upstairs. Simon put the drink into Walter's hand then went to answer the phone. It was the private number which was only known to his most senior colleagues in Government. Simon recognized the voice immediately. 'Yes, sir,' he said, then nodded stupidly at the receiver and began to wave frantically at Walter. When he finally noticed, Walter padded sadly across.

'It's the First Minister,' Simon said, and whatever blood was left in Walter's face drained away.

Walter put the phone against his chest, took a deep breath, then raised it to his mouth. 'First Minister?' he asked querulously.

Simon just made out a familiar, 'Walter, how are you bearing up?' as he retreated back to the kitchen to make himself a cup of tea.

Walter was ordered to resign his seat, and within the hour he did.

Within two hours Tara came down the stairs, with cases packed. Despite Walter's pleadings she refused to leave along the back lane. Instead she brazenly opened the front door and asked the assembled press to help her lift her belongings into her Land Cruiser. They were more than eager, and didn't even resume shouting their questions until the boot was firmly closed and Tara was climbing into the driver's seat.

'Have you anything to say, Mrs Adair?'

'Only that I won't be Mrs Adair for much longer.'

'Are you getting divorced?'

'What do you bloody think, Sherlock?' she snapped.

And then she was off, with photographers chasing her down the drive.

*   *   *

Shortly before midnight, Simon said he would have to go. His boyfriend was waiting. Walter, deathly pale and very drunk, didn't even register the confession. He said blearily, 'Y'know, the half of it isn't true.'

'But what about the other half?' Simon asked, with the courage of the drink.

Walter shook his head sadly. 'I love her,' he said.

9

It is a little-known fact that, outside of the United States, more baseball bats are sold in Belfast than in any other city in the world. What is even more remarkable is the fact that there is no baseball league in Belfast. In fact there are no baseball teams. There aren't even any *baseballs* for sale. Just the bats.

Professor Simmington was telling Ruth this as they walked along the corridor to his office. She'd already been kept waiting for over an hour on what was now the second day of Harry's stay in the Royal Victoria Hospital, that vast crumbling edifice that sits regally on the edge of Republican West Belfast.

Harry had not regained consciousness. They had been running tests on him for the past twenty-four hours and keeping the results to themselves. Ruth had been fobbed off with evasive responses and platitudes. She was half convinced they were conspiring against her. They wouldn't even let her in to see him, and told her obvious lies about the possibility of his having some obscure communicable disease.

'Aye,' Ruth had responded bitterly, 'what is it, a wee touch of Black Death?' and they'd looked ashen-faced at her, shocked at her callousness. Ruth didn't care. They knew him as that roly-poly television chef with a smile for everyone. She despised him as the philandering bastard who'd ruined her life. Later, when she'd calmed down, she was angry at herself. She apologized to the nurses. She bought them a box of Milk Tray and they sat through the night with her, wary yet, but gradually warming to her, although not enough to eat the black cherry. She started to tell them about how awful Harry was, but then stopped. They had guessed it, anyway. So she told them instead about the famous people she had met and been disappointed by.

Eventually, the following day, the top man summoned her. She was absolutely determined to get answers. And not just answers – *results*! The Professor, in turn, was doing his best to reassure Ruth that when it came to acts of violence there was no better place for her husband to be. 'We've had so much practice,' he grinned, 'what we don't know about gunshot wounds you could write on the head of a bullet.'

'He hasn't been shot, Professor,' Ruth said dryly. He ignored her. He continued to rabbit away about the beatings the local paramilitaries doled out to locals who got out of line. 'They've found, the paramilitaries that is, that the baseball bat is the perfect instrument with which to inflict a kind of controlled damage. It's particularly good for breaking limbs, a nice clean fracture, you see. It's not as bloody as a machete and doesn't require a power source like a chainsaw. In fact, it's so painless and easy, some of them have taken to breaking their own legs and claiming the compensation . . .'

'Professor?'

He looked at her for a moment, and seemed frankly surprised that she was there at all. 'I'm sorry. Of course. Where was I? Your husband.' He was large and full of himself, Ruth thought, and why not, he was a healer, an instrument of God. If Harry was an instrument of God, she decided, he was a set of bagpipes. Annoying, and full of wind.

Professor Simmington's office was small and untidy. Ruth collapsed into a chair, exhausted. Between the hours spent at the hospital and tossing and turning at home, convinced that Harry was up and charming the knickers off the nurses, she'd hardly slept at all. Claire had come round, and Billy had done what he could, but what could either of them do? Their father was unconscious or feigning it in the hospital. 'At least it's quiet,' Billy had said the night before, sitting with her in the kitchen. She'd nodded. It was. As it should be. As it *would* be.

She blinked back into the Professor's misplaced grin. '. . . Of course I'm here all day, but I have to confess I get my wife to tape his shows. Fancy myself as a bit of a dab hand in the kitchen . . .'

'What exactly is wrong with him, Professor?'

The Professor pursed his lips, then turned and examined a series of X-rays displayed behind him.

Ruth came up and stood by his side. 'Sorry,' she said, 'it's just . . .'

'I understand.' He nodded thoughtfully for several moments, then drew his large, dark fingers across the surface of the X-rays. 'The brain,' he said, 'is a wonderful instrument.'

'When it works,' Ruth said.

He smiled. 'But it is also wholly unpredictable. Think of it as a protective measure. Shutting him down until it has a chance to repair itself, or until danger has passed. The way a hedgehog curls itself into a little ball.'

Did he think she was simple or something? Or a child? *A hedgehog? Well, he had turned into a right prick.*

She could feel the anger, and the tears, welling up in her. She bit at her lip to stop herself saying something. It wasn't his fault.

It was Harry's.

A few more minutes of mundane, child-friendly explanation, then she was being ushered along the plain blue, shiny corridor towards the Special Care Unit. The Professor stopped just outside the door and gave her a reassuring smile. She knew there wouldn't be anything in there to surprise her. Just Harry asleep on a bed, trying desperately not to laugh.

The Professor stepped to one side and Ruth took her first proper look at Harry since he'd pulled his stunt in the courtroom.

Immediately she felt her legs go weak. She might have collapsed if the Professor hadn't put out his arm for her to steady herself against.

Harry.

Harry . . .

The pipes. The tubes. The monitors. The drips. The callow, sallow, saggy, lifeless, hopeless look of the rotund, fleshy, scatter-haired, dank-faced man who was so nearly not her husband.

Harry.

I hate you but by Jesus you look rough.

'It's a coma, Mrs McKee,' the Professor said gently.

When she had recovered herself a little, Ruth managed to ask, 'How long?' but the Professor just gave a little shrug and said, 'Who can tell?'

An hour later, after a good stiff drink, Ruth was replaying the scene in Ms Boyle's office. The initial shock had worn off. It had been replaced by anger and resentment. Pretty much the way her life had been lived since Harry had turned into a prick.

'It's a coma, Mrs McKee. Who can tell?' she echoed.

'I'm very sorry, Ruth,' said Boyle.

'*I'm* very sorry,' Ruth shot back. 'This bollockses things up, doesn't it?'

Boyle nodded. 'It could delay the divorce indefinitely.' She sighed. 'I'm sorry, Ruth, it's just the way of the world. I'm afraid the comatose often have the final word.'

It could be weeks, months, years . . . *longer*. She wouldn't be able to sell the property. Harry's bank account could be frozen. JJ might fight her every step of the way, bankrupt her. It was okay for him, he was a solicitor already, he could do it all for nothing, or for Harry. Ruth shook her head bitterly. 'But what if they can't bring him round?'

Silence hung mournfully in the pristine office.

Then Ruth, wiping her eyes, saw a look on her solicitor's face that surprised her. She was sitting back in her immaculate leather chair and staring out of the window. But her eyes weren't focused on anything. They were lost in space. Ruth had expected a sympathetic look, or perhaps one of cold calculation, but what she saw instead was a kind of defiant glow. Boyle was nodding to herself. She began to drum a felt tip pen against the palm of her hand. 'But what if they can't bring him round?' she repeated slowly, then finally turned her gaze back onto Ruth. 'Then *you're* going to have to.'

'*What*?' Ruth said.

Boyle was up out of her chair. She hammered her fist onto the desk. '*You*, Ruth. *You* can't let him get away with it. *You* need to wake him up. And not just for yourself, for all of us.'

10

It was as if he had spent his life climbing to the very top of the highest mountain, only to lose his footing on the summit and go slipping down the other side, getting faster and faster and faster as he fell, aware that nothing could stop him, that there was one single, inevitable conclusion.

Walter Adair hadn't slept, he hadn't eaten. He was still taking liquids. Vodka, mainly. He was drunk *and* he had a hangover. He had been resigned from the party. He was a political pariah. In fact, he was just a pariah full stop. Everyone had loved him, and now everyone hated him. Worse – they were laughing at him. Somewhere, in the fog, he remembered trying to order a pizza by phone, but the guy hadn't been able to stop laughing for long enough to take the order. Political downfall isn't usually enough to provoke hysterics in pizza boys, and it puzzled Walter for some minutes, until one of the gang of reporters still stationed outside the house thoughtfully pushed a copy of *The Sun* through the letterbox. The tabloid, as it often did, had some hint of nudity on the front with a promise of further pictures within, but Walter flicked past, looking for something about himself. *The Sun* had always been good to him. It was read by the man in the street, in the building site, in the civil service, in the pub, and Walter had gone out of his way to build a relationship with it. He even wrote an occasional column for it. It could make you, and it could break you. And now it was breaking Walter into little pieces. With a sudden sense of dread he flicked back to the front. Yes, indeed, he recognized those buttocks. The headline read BARE-FACED CHEEK – and in smaller letters, but with a big red star around them: *Walter Adair's Nude Romp with Hairdresser, see centre pages.* Walter saw the centre pages and wept. It had just been a bit of fun. A laugh. Nobody was supposed to get hurt, least of all him. People didn't understand. Tara had never been keen on sex. Once a week, tops. He had needs, he had urges, what harm . . . *Tomorrow – I Was a Top Jockey Until Walter Took Me for a Ride*. Walter gasped. There was a photo

of a boy who hardly looked more than fifteen. Christ!
How to explain that, how to fucking explain that!
Sure, there'd been a jockey, but he was well into his
twenties when they'd met. *He'd* seduced Walter. It
hadn't lasted more than a couple of minutes. Christ!

They listened in on the way over to the hospital.
Ruth driving, Claire beside her, and Billy in the back
cradling the ghetto blaster.

'This is bloody madness,' Billy was saying. 'This is
never going to bring him round.'

'It's a start, Billy,' said Claire, 'it's something. I
don't hear any brighter ideas from you.'

'I was thinking electric shock.'

'Billy.'

'Or leeches. Apparently they're back in fashion.
Stick him in a bath of leeches. They'll probably hail
the return of a long-lost brother.'

'Billy.' Ruth gave him a look in the mirror, and
then called for quiet as she turned the radio up.

*'Tonight the downward spiral of rising politician Walter
Adair continues to gain pace,'* the newsreader intoned
gravely. *'His resignation was swiftly followed by his wife's
departure and then this evening more drama. We'll go over
to Tim Burton who's on the Queen Elizabeth Bridge in the
dockland area of East Belfast . . . Tim, what's been
happening?'*

'Well, Sean, high drama indeed. Mr Adair had been a virtual prisoner in his Hillsborough house overnight with literally dozens of press keeping a round-the-clock vigil. Despite repeated requests for interviews there was no communication from the now former Assemblyman. The first indication that anything was up came at around five this morning when the darkness was suddenly cut by the sound of Winston Churchill . . .'

'Winston Churchill, Tim?'

'Yes, Clive. His recorded speeches, and at very high volume. Scared the living daylights out of us at first. It was very much "fight them on the beaches", so we were, as it were, primed for something. Then at nearly six this morning, with Churchill still booming around us, the front door opened and Mr Adair emerged, looking, it must be said, a little the worse for wear.'

'And then what happened?'

'Well, Clive, Mr Adair let loose with some choice language towards the members of the press, which I'm afraid we can't broadcast . . .'

'Damn,' said Billy.

'Shhhh,' said Ruth. They pulled into the hospital car park, but they sat there, the rain smacking off the windscreen, while they listened to Walter's freefall.

'Mr Adair then made his way to his white Toyota Land Cruiser, and drove off.'

'In his . . . would you say, "inebriated" state?'

'He certainly gave that appearance, Clive, and his driving might best be described as erratic. However, the press pack weren't just going to let him drive off, and so something of a chase through the city began.'

'Do we know where he was trying to go?'

'Well, he was heading for Belfast. He only made one stop on the way, and that was at an Xtravision video store in Lisburn to leave back several videotapes.'

'Do we know what those titles were, Tim?'

'No.'

'Okay, then what happened?'

'After that Mr Adair drove into Belfast and spent almost half an hour trying to shake off the following press pack. But of course with satellite tracking now almost de rigueur, that's almost impossible these days. He did at one point stop the car, get out and approach the first of the following vehicles. He was seen to be carrying a can of what appeared to be de-icer. Somewhat fearful of his demeanour, the occupants of the car refused to wind down their window, at which point Mr Adair attempted to spray the vehicle with the de-icer but could not seem to get it to work. He threw the can away, then screamed at the many cars that had now stopped to watch that he had had enough and that they should leave him alone.'

'It must be very difficult to be under that constant gaze, Tim.'

'Yes, Clive, it is in some respects reprehensible, but we must also remember that this is a man who has courted the press, sought them out, who has in many respects built his career through them; he cannot have expected them just to turn a blind eye to his behaviour.'

'So what happened then, Tim?'

'Well, Clive, Mr Adair returned to his vehicle, and the press continued their pursuit as far as the Queen Elizabeth Bridge, where I am now. It was here that Mr Adair suddenly pulled over, leapt out of his car and dashed towards the edge of the bridge itself with reporters and photographers in pursuit. Mr Adair reached the protective railings, pulled himself up onto the top of them, looked back once at the press pack and then hurled himself towards the freezing waters far below.'

'Jesus,' Ruth said.

'Daddy strikes again,' said Billy from the back.

'Shhhh,' said Claire.

'Mr Adair would almost certainly have drowned, if it hadn't been for the cargo barge passing below. The former Assemblyman hit the deck with considerable force and is thought to have sustained serious injuries. Paramedics were on the scene within thirty minutes and Mr Adair was rushed to hospital. We've not had any more news, but we're expecting . . .'

Ruth switched the radio off. Claire said, 'He couldn't sue Daddy, could he? For starting it all?'

Ruth shrugged.

'Don't be daft,' Billy said. 'He'd have to wheel coma boy into court. Dad would have to give evidence through a medium.'

'Could you put a cork in it, Billy?' Ruth asked. 'Just for five minutes?'

'Five? Okay.'

'Thanks.' They got out of the car, and dashed through the rain to the hospital. They shook themselves off and began walking along the corridor.

'Four minutes and ten seconds, four minutes and nine seconds, four minutes and eight . . .'

'Billy, shut up.'

'Four minutes and seven seconds . . .'

'*Billy!*'

Harry had been moved out of intensive care into a private room within a larger ward. He was still hooked up to this, that and everything, but Ruth didn't find it half so upsetting. Claire was a bit tearful, but Billy just looked blankly at him, then turned his attention to the Gameboy he'd brought with him.

A nurse stopped in the doorway. She had a large plastic bag in her hand. 'Oh . . . Mrs McKee . . . what do you want me to do with these?' She held the bag up. Ruth's brow crinkled. The nurse reached in and removed a handful of garishly coloured envelopes. 'Get well cards,' she said, 'we've hundreds of them.'

'Oh . . .' Ruth shook her head helplessly. 'I don't know.'

'He's a popular man.'

'Yes, isn't he just? Would you just hold on to them, until . . .?'

'Sure.'

Billy smiled up at the nurse. 'Is there any chocolates, or gifts, anything like that . . .?'

'*Billy!*'

The nurse smiled and retreated. Billy rolled his eyes and returned his attention to his computer game. Claire set about organizing the music. The theory was: play music he likes, talk to him, remind him of things, you never know what might get through, help get his brain kick-started again. Ruth had no idea what Harry's current musical tastes were, but they'd grown up in the same era, they were teenagers in the early seventies when Glam was all the rage. She knew from the long nights she spent alone in her bedroom with the music coming through the dividing wall that Harry still turned to the old stuff when he came home drunk and wanting to cheer himself up. So it was back to the seventies. Flares and perms.

David Bowie: *The Man Who Fell to Earth*. 'Ziggy

Stardust'. 'Star Man'. 'Five Years'. Steve Harley and Cockney Rebel: 'Make Me Smile (Come Up and See Me)'. Sparks: 'This Town Ain't Big Enough for the Both of Us'. Slade. Roxy Music. The Velvet Underground. Jimmy Hendrix. God, stuff she hadn't listened to in years, yet they used to be so passionate about it.

'If you were playing this stuff to me,' Billy said, 'I'd stay unconscious.'

Claire slapped his head playfully and sang along to the Rubettes. She tried to get Ruth to join in and she went along half-heartedly for a few lines, but then gave up. Claire trailed off as well, then stood looking sadly at her mother. She knelt beside her and took her hand. 'Mum, you have to talk to him. If you want him to wake up, you have to talk to him.'

'What about?' Ruth said. But she knew. Of course she knew. Claire smiled encouragingly. Ruth shrugged. *This is embarrassing. In front of my own kids.*

'Hold on,' Claire said. She jumped up and turned the lights off. They were left with just the vague greenish light and rhythmic blip-blip from Harry's monitors and the occasional echoey hospital sound from the corridor outside. Billy tutted and angled his Gameboy closer to the monitor, but otherwise they sat quietly in the dark and watched Harry. His breathing wasn't being assisted any more. The bruises were healing. He looked for all the world like he was just sleeping, and there was at least a part of Ruth that was convinced that he was.

'Go on, Mum,' Claire said gently.

Ruth took a deep breath. 'Do you remember . . .?' She stopped and shuffled her chair closer to the bed. She hesitated for a moment, then took Harry's hand. She gave it a little squeeze. It was cool and fleshy. She half expected him to suddenly squeeze back, really hard, but there was nothing, no pressure at all. 'Do you remember,' she began again, 'when we first met, Harry? The beach party, and we had the big flagons of cider? Do you remember that?' She paused, waiting for a response. 'You walked me home along the beach, and we were messing about that much my shoes floated out to sea. I had to walk home in my bare feet and when we got there, you washed them for me. I told you it was the most romantic thing anyone had ever done, and you said, no, it was the bravest.' Ruth smiled briefly at the memory of it. She looked at Claire. 'Long time ago,' she said.

The tape was changed. Another. An hour passed.

Ruth began to get into it, in a strange way. Telling a story. Like *Jackanory*, though Claire, sitting back in her chair enjoying every minute of it, hadn't a clue what *Jackanory* was. Billy had dropped off to sleep.

'God, and then the wedding. I organized the whole bloody thing; it was great. I could have organized the Normandy landings, the form I was in, and all you had to do, the only damn thing you had to do was organize the music for me to walk down the aisle to. Remember? The registry office. Tiny wee place. All you had to do was provide enough romantic music for me to walk about ten yards. You promised. You *promised.*' Ruth let out another laugh. 'Claire, I swear to God, I didn't intend to be late, but sure isn't it a woman's prerogative? I was only about twenty minutes behind schedule, my bloody dress got caught in the roses outside my dad's, and then m'dad wanted to drive round the town showing off his beautiful daughter. Ha!' She shook her head. 'You'd think Harry might have thought of that. Allowed a little extra time. But oh, no. Not Harry. He had this cassette player all set up at the front of the registry office, and right on the hour, JJ switched it on. No sign of me yet, but JJ switched it on. He was doing best man – did I say that?' Claire shook her head and smiled. 'Anyway, I roll up twenty minutes late. Just as I come to the door, just as I start walking down the aisle, the bloody tape ends, JJ flips over the cassette and presses play. And this blushing bride walks down the aisle to "All Shook Up" by Elvis Presley.' They were both cackling with laughter then. 'You should have seen my face on the home movie, like bloody thunder.' She paused and looked sadly at Harry. 'Great day though.'

Long time ago, she thought again.

The music went on. They were into Yes, into Led Zeppelin. How long had they been there? *Nearly three hours*. Jesus.

Claire had dozed off in her chair as well. Ruth stared at Harry again. At his closed, pouched eyes. His sallow complexion. His dank hair. His cracked lips.

She remembered the honeymoon. They went to the Isle of Man. They walked on the beach. She had always loved beaches. The sea. Could never have lived inland. They drank and they made love and she was the happiest girl in the world. Then she was pregnant and Harry started working on TV. The money was coming in. Harry was being stopped in the street. They thought it was great. They were invited out all the time, but then there were difficulties with the pregnancy and she couldn't go out as much, though she didn't mind Harry going because it was work, and it was play, and he deserved it – he had worked hard. She never stopped him. Never said, no, don't go, Harry.

The pregnancy. That's where it started to go wrong. She was mean and she was moody and she was self-contained. She just wanted to be alone. She was scared. It was all new to her. She wanted to lock the door and not let anyone in. She certainly didn't want to make love. It was better that Harry was out enjoying himself. One night she ate a piece of coal.

'Do you remember, Harry, in the delivery room and the pain was horrendous and the surgeon said, *Everything will be okay, Mrs McKee*, and I said, thank you, doctor, I know it will, and then you were there and you said, *Everything will be okay*, and I told you to piss off and die, what the fuck did you know about the pain . . . and then there she was, our little Claire, and that killer smile and those gorgeous eyes . . .'

She squeezed his hand. She looked at Claire. She looked at Billy. How it might have been if he hadn't screwed it all away. Well, it was too late. He had ruined it, ruined everything. He was lying helpless in bed and he was still managing to screw her life up. She needed him up. She needed him walking and talking. She let go of his hand. She had tears in her eyes.

'GET UP, YOU LAZY BASTARD!' she screamed.

Claire and Billy jumped up, startled and confused, as Ruth collapsed down into her seat. She was crying hard. Claire put her arm round her. 'It's okay,' she said. 'Dad's going to be okay.'

Ruth nodded against her. He was going to be okay. He was going to get better, and he was going to move out of the house. They would be divorced. Life would start again. It would be okay.

11

Dead silence. Unable to sleep, Ruth tosses and turns. She sweats. Her heart thumps. She always tries to doze off on happy thoughts, but the happy thoughts she has are all too familiar, they have been called upon far too often. She needs new happy thoughts. She tries to focus on the future, on getting a new job, on sorting out the house, on Claire's graduation, on Billy maturing into the fine young man she knows is in there beneath the cheeky wee monkey. She turns left, she turns right. She tries lying on her back. She changes to her stomach. Nothing will work. Yet she's so utterly tired. Her arms and legs ache. The room is hot, she opens a window. The breeze is cold and the crash of the waves against the sea wall is far from soothing. She seeks out her CD Walkman and nestles under the quilt listening to the Beatles. The red greatest hits. She tries to imagine that Paul McCartney is serenading her with 'Yesterday'. Then what John Lennon was like in bed. She remembers being in the bath when she was a girl and singing along with her dad to 'Yellow Submarine' while he shaved at the sink. They don't write songs like that any more. She is just beginning to drift off when there's a sudden change in the light and she opens her eyes, blinks against the brightness, and Billy is standing there in the doorway. She says 'WHAT?' far too loudly while she searches for the off button. Then a slightly scrambled, 'Sorry . . . what . . . what is it?'

'The hospital called.'

Her heart is thump-thump-thumping. 'Hosp – your dad . . .?' Billy is looking at her. His face is pale, blank. 'Billy . . .?'

'I'm afraid' – and he leaves it lingering in the air for a moment that seems to stretch into an hour – 'I'm afraid Fatboy Slim is out of his coma.'

'He's . . .?'

'Yeah. He woke up an hour ago and demanded a battered sausage.'

She never did get over to sleep again. When Billy woke, late for school already, he found his mother in Harry's room desperately crushing his belongings into suitcases and travel bags, even plastic bags. There was a kind of frenzied desperation about it. 'What're you doing?' Billy said, asking the bloody obvious.

Ruth barely paused. 'If he thinks he's coming home here, he's in for a big surprise.'

And he was, just not quite what Ruth had in mind.

Harry was indeed awake. He'd been dreaming about football, about scoring a goal at Wembley for United. Denis Law centring, Bobby Charlton nodding it on, then Harry volleying it into the net. And George Best buying him a drink in the bar later. Harry loved football. It was lush. He wanted up and out of bed, but the nurses were adamant that he couldn't move about until the doctor had spoken to him. Nurses! They were all really nice. Pretty. Every time he said something they smiled at him. Really made him feel like he was the centre of attention. He asked them several times what he was doing in the hospital at all. He couldn't quite work it out. He had felt his arms and his legs and they were fine. There were painful spots on his face, sure, but nothing that serious. Maybe he'd come off his bike, cracked his head. Yeah, that would be it.

Then the doctor came. A black fella. Harry was trying to remember if he'd ever actually spoken to a black fella before. There were hardly any in Belfast. Not even at uni.

'Morning, Harry,' the doctor said. Harry smiled and nodded. The nurse was grinning at him. She fancied him, clearly. 'Bit of a knock on the head,' the doctor was saying. Harry nodded along. The nurse was blushing under his gaze. 'You've been unconscious for, oh, nearly six days. Now, let's see if everything is working.'

He began to flex Harry's arms and legs. It wasn't actually painful, it was just like they were really tired, like he'd run a marathon. 'I feel very . . .'

'You will,' the doctor said, then nodded, lifted the chart at the foot of his bed and made a note. 'Now, I want you to raise your hand . . . uhuh . . . Now see if you can touch the end of your nose . . .'

Harry was doing his best to take it seriously, but it was all so daft. He held his hand out before him, then slowly moved a finger towards his nose. At the last moment he deliberately veered it off and pretended to poke himself in the eye. The nurse, suckered in, jumped to see if he was all right. The doctor just shook his head. Harry winked at her and she blushed again. Then he touched his nose properly. Once, twice, three times.

'Tell me,' the doctor said, 'what's the capital of France.'

'F.'

The doctor smiled. 'Very good, Harry. Now, what's your full name?'

'Harry McKee. What's yours, doctor?'

'Professor. Professor Simmington.'

'Oh . . .' Harry nodded, mock-impressed.

'Where do you live, Harry?'

'Marlborough Park.' Professor Simmington's brow furrowed slightly as he checked the address on the file. It didn't match. Harry McKee lived in Donaghadee, not in Belfast. 'Where do you live?' Harry asked.

'I live here, Harry, to look after you.' The Professor nodded thoughtfully. 'How old are you, Harry?' he asked.

'Eighteen.'

Harry was pissed off. There wasn't a bloody thing wrong with him, yet they'd absolutely forbidden him to get out of bed. They wouldn't even lend him a newspaper. There had been a small radio beside the bed but a gruff workie in blue overalls had come and removed it, grunting something about it needing fixing. He had asked about visiting time, about when his mum or dad or Ruth or someone would come to relieve the monotony. Even the nurses didn't seem half as friendly now. The little one with the blush avoided his eyes every time he said something and when he asked if it was okay for him to go to the toilet she had looked horrified and rushed away. A starchy matron had arrived a few moments later and escorted him past what he took to be the normal bathroom and down a corridor to a door marked STAFF ONLY, and there showed him a tiny room with a single toilet in it, a small washbasin, but no mirror. All the way there, and all the way back, people were looking at him oddly.

'What's wrong, have I got the plague or something?' he asked, but old poker face just snorted *No* and escorted him back to his bed.

Harry knew he couldn't have anything that was *really* contagious, otherwise he wouldn't have been allowed out of his room, but there was definitely something weird going on. For a start, he wasn't out in the general ward, he was in a room by himself. And his folks would *never* pay for something private. That said, it wasn't exactly private either. There were two large windows on either side of it. The men in the rest of the ward seemed to find it very entertaining to stand and stare at him. One cupped his hands against the glass and shouted, 'What's cooking?'

at him. 'I don't know,' Harry shouted back. 'They haven't said.' They seemed to find that very funny, and Harry laughed back and gave them the thumbs-up, but underneath it frightened him a little. He asked the nurse to pull the curtains and he pretended to go to sleep.

He was actually starting to drift when he heard the surprised voice of the little red-faced nurse just outside his room. 'Ruth,' she was saying, 'I thought they would have caught you down below . . .'

Ruth?

At last.

But then there were footsteps, and the nurse's voice trailing off with, 'Isn't it wonderful? Last night he just woke up . . .'

Ruth. Beautiful, sexy, marvellous Ruth.

He waited five minutes, then ten, for her to return. But there was no sign of her. Bloody hell. What were they playing at? They were treating him like a child.

Professor Simmington had been breaking bad news for years, he was an old hand at it and he rarely got flustered. He was calm, he was soft spoken, he was reassuring, he was sympathetic, yet Ruth had him flummoxed. He didn't quite know where to pitch it. She seemed angry, unsure of what she actually wanted to hear.

'Ruth, the brain is a wonderful . . .'

'. . . Instrument. Yes, I know. I have this feeling of *déjà* vu. Or maybe I've just heard it all before.'

'Wonderful but temperamental. Ruth, we have people here who have been through considerably less trauma than your husband, people who have healed physically yet their minds are . . .' Her eyes told him that she didn't want the bullshit version, and he trailed off. They looked at each other for several long moments. 'He's lost his memory, Ruth.' There was no response. Her eyes were darting about. There were a hundred conflicting emotions in there. He moved the soothing voice down a gear. 'Sometimes a patient can't even remember how to lift a spoon, or comb his hair, sometimes he can't even remember how to swallow.' He smiled optimistically at her, then moved the voice back up again. 'Much more common is a partial amnesia, where a particular memory block is excised by the trauma of . . .'

'How much does he remember?' Ruth cut in sharply.

There was a slight disbelieving curl to her upper lip. If she'd been a soldier on D-Day, the Professor thought, she wouldn't have taken any prisoners. He folded his hands before him. *Just the facts, ma'am.* 'He doesn't know he's married. He thinks he's eighteen.'

She raised her head slightly, and her eyes bored into him, searching for the trace of a smile, for the hint of a concealed laugh scratching to get out, but he remained perfectly composed. 'What?' she said.

'He doesn't know he's married. He thinks he's eighteen.'

She took a deep breath. 'You've got to be kidding.'

'I'm sorry, Ruth.'

'You've got to be fucking kidding.'

He cleared his throat. The best thing was to move on, that way she'd realize he was perfectly serious. 'Ruth,' he said with quiet authority, 'it's going to be a slow process. You'll just have to go with the flow, not take it personally. He has a lot to come to terms with, and not just mentally, but physically as well. So it's the kid glove treatment for a while.' He wasn't sure how much of it reached her. She was shaking her head. 'As for the TV stuff, well, I think we'd better put that on the back burner for a while, best not to overload the system, eh?'

She was still staring at him. 'Are you taking the friggin' hand out of me?'

'Ruth . . . honestly.'

'He's lost his memory?'

'Part of it, he . . .'

'He thinks he's eighteen?'

'Yes, he . . .'

'He doesn't know he's bloody married?'

'No, he . . .'

'Bloody hell.'

They sat nodding at each other for a while. She started to say something several times, then decided against it. She looked beyond him, behind him. He couldn't quite tell where her eyes were focused, but he suspected she was studying his framed qualifications to be sure they were authentic.

'Ruth, I . . .'

'Can you categorically assure me that he's not just friggin' about?'

He called up the reassuring smile. 'Ruth, I am ninety-nine per cent certain that your husband is not' – and at that moment his eyes fell on Harry's face, pressed up close against the office door, his nostrils bent up and back like a pig's, his breath misting up the glass, his fingers behind his ears, pressing them forward, flapping, a big stupid smile plastered across his face – 'just . . . friggin' . . . about . . .'

Ruth's eyes followed his, and locked quickly onto Harry. Even for her husband, it was a new low in buffoonery. Her face grew cold, her eyes stern.

Harry, on the other hand, was immediately confused. He'd expected Ruth's happy giggle – here he was SAFE AND WELL – but all he felt was foolish. There was some old woman sitting there scowling at him. He'd gotten the wrong room. He disengaged from the glass with as much decorum as a man doing a Percy Pig routine to a complete stranger can. He should have checked first. He should have . . . and yet . . . God, if she wasn't just like Ruth's mother. In fact, the eyes were . . . Harry straightened. He peered through the glass again. She was looking at him oddly. Behind her that professor was slowly rising up out of his chair. Harry looked back at the woman. God, she must be in her forties but she was so totally familiar, yet in a way he couldn't quite grasp . . .

Harry opened the door, determined to get a better look.

'It's okay, Harry,' the Professor said, coming towards him now, his hands held out before him. 'Just keep looking at me.'

But he couldn't, he was looking at the woman, at the familiar eyes and unfamiliar scowl. She began to move up out of her seat, but the professor had a hand on her shoulder. 'Just stay where you are, Ruth, I'll deal with this . . .'

'Ruth . . .?' Harry said.

He sounded so incredulous.

'Ruth?' Harry said again. He was studying her face,

her hands, her legs. If it really was her, something dreadful must have . . . 'Oh, my God. What happened to you?'

'To me?' Ruth snapped angrily.

'Harry,' the professor was saying, 'it's okay. Just keep looking at me . . .'

But Harry was backing away, out of the door, his hand rubbing at his forehead, his legs feeling weak and wasted. 'I don't understand . . . I don't . . .' As he looked about him, confused, his eyes fell suddenly on the fire doors beside Professor Simmington's office. There was an old man staring at him from the other side of the glass. Harry threw up his hands in despair. 'Stop staring at me!' he yelled and pushed at the door, but there was no one there. As the door swung shut again the old man reappeared. Harry put his hand to his mouth, so did the old man.

'Harry, please, just come with me . . .'

Harry stepped closer to the door. It was his reflection. He pawed at it, but pawed only at himself.

A tremor shook him. His legs buckled beneath him. He tried to make a grab for the door but missed. The professor knelt beside him as he crumpled onto the linoleum tiles, but Harry's eyes, wide and imploring, sought only Ruth.

'Ruth . . . Ruth . . .' he cried, his voice full of

panic and desperation, 'what's happening to us? What's happening to us?'

But she was looking away.

Harry closed his eyes. He began to rock himself, there on the cold hospital floor, with the other patients staring out of their wards at him, with the black professor hugging him, with the girl he loved old and wrinkled before him; he rocked and he rocked and he rocked, willing himself to wake up.

Wake up, Harry! Wake up!

12

Ruth didn't want to go in to see him. He was back in his room. They'd given him tranquillizers. But he was still as perky as a virgin on a promise. Professor Simmington spent a long time in there with him, trying to explain, trying to make him understand that he wasn't really eighteen, that Ruth hadn't turned into some oul' doll overnight any more than he had.

'Does he believe you?' Ruth asked when the Professor eventually tracked her down in the cafeteria.

'He thinks I'm a space cadet.' The professor smiled, then sat opposite her. He didn't need an invitation. It was his hospital, up to a point. He had a coffee already, and a plate of biscuits. 'He understands what I'm telling him. It's not the same as *understanding*, if you understand what I'm getting at. German biscuit?'

'What?'

'Would you like a German biscuit?'

'No . . . thank you.' Ruth's coffee was long cold. Her nails were bitten to the quick. She felt old. She'd spent ten minutes in the ladies looking at her face. Her old face. She'd seen the horror in Harry's eyes when he'd realized who she was. *I'm not old*, she told herself, *Harry made me this way*. But then she thought, *no, I am old, I'm middle-aged*.

'You're not old,' Professor Simmington said.

'What . . .?'

'You're not old. I know what you're thinking. I've been through this a dozen times, Ruth. Harry's seeing everything through an eighteen-year-old's eyes, you think he thinks you're an old woman, but whatever he thinks, you're not.'

'I'm middle-aged.'

'No, you're not.'

'I'm forty. If I'm lucky I'll live to eighty. Forty is half of eighty. If I only live to sixty I'm already two thirds of the way there.'

The professor sighed. 'You can't go in there with that attitude.'

'I'm not going in there at all.'

'Yes, you are. You can't not go in there. He's your husband, and he needs your help to get through this.'

'We're getting divorced. But for this, we would have been divorced. All I want is him out of my life.'

'All he wants is to understand his life, and only you can help him to do that.'

'That's not fair.'

'Life's not fair, Ruth.'

And don't I bloody know it? Ruth sighed. She tutted. 'What am I supposed to do? The truth, the whole truth or nothing like the truth?'

'Use your own good judgement.'

'If I'd used my own good judgement I . . .' She trailed off. What was the point? She checked her watch. She'd phoned Claire and asked her to call round to the house to pick up their wedding album. That would be a start. But there was no sign of her, and that had been a couple of hours ago. She tried Claire's mobile again after the professor left, but it was switched off. *Shit.*

She knew she couldn't put it off any longer. She had to face him. Her mind raced as she walked back to Harry's ward. If he really had lost his memory, how much to tell him? The full monty, or the edited highlights? The professor had already advised her to steer clear of revealing his television background, so that kind of limited her, but how not to let fly with what she really felt?

They hadn't had a really serious stand-up row in years.

It was all bottled up.

It had all been about silence.

Like living in a freezer.

She paused outside his room, looked at him through the glass. He was sitting there tucked up in bed like a four-year-old, his pinball eyes darting madly about. Not that there was anything for him to get excited about. The room was empty of all the things she had come to associate with Harry: newspapers, books, television, drink, betting slips, sausages. She had fantasized about taking them all away from him before, as a last desperate measure, but had come to the conclusion that it would be like removing his skeleton. He had become those things, and without them he would be fatally diminished, he would be reduced to a puddle of fat. It wasn't the material things that she needed to remove from Harry, it was herself.

He caught her eye, standing there at the glass, and smiled.

She smiled weakly and entered the room. She stood with her arms folded, and looked everywhere, but at her husband. His eyes were drinking in every inch of her, she could feel them rolling up and down her like midnight slugs. She snapped, 'Will you quit staring at me?'

'Sorry . . . you've changed . . . you . . .'

'Yeah, well, you're no oil painting yourself.'

'I didn't mean . . . I just . . . I don't remember . . . nobody's telling me anything. I don't know what's going on . . . What is this, *Twenty Questions*?'

'What?'

'I was going to university, did I graduate, what do I do, what did I become?'

Test one. 'We both went. You studied politics.' *Why not tell him? Just tell him what a shit he is. Like he doesn't already know. Like he's not faking it.* 'You became . . . you interview. You interview politicians. People in the news.'

'Really?'

'Really.'

'Lush.' She was on the verge of jumping in with, *And you make an arse of yourself every morning on local television*, but he surprised her with a sudden interest in someone other than himself. 'And you? What did you become . . .?'

She shrugged. 'Oh, this and that. A mother.'

'A mother? You mean kids?' She nodded. 'What are they?'

'Trouble.' She looked at him and gave a little laugh.

His face was a picture. A luminous picture. She thought for the briefest moment how wonderful it would be to be able to forget all the crap that had gone before. To start again. Before he could ask anything else the door opened and a nurse looked in. Ruth, happy for the distraction, smiled at her.

'Can I get youse a wee cup of tea?' she asked. There was a trolley behind her.

Ruth nodded, then turned back to Harry. He gave an embarrassed shrug. 'This is silly – I don't even know if I drink tea. I didn't used to but now . . .?'

He looked to Ruth for help.

'Yes, of course you do.' And it struck her suddenly: 'Since you gave up the drink.'

Ruth nodded at the nurse. They remained silent while she brought the cups in, and waited until she'd closed the door behind her before continuing. Harry's voice was lower, his eyes full of disappointment. 'Was I bad with it? The drink?'

Ruth nodded, but said, 'No, not really.'

'What does that mean?'

'Harry . . .'

'What does it mean? Was I bad with it or not?'

'Harry, the doctor said . . .'

'Nobody's telling me anything.'

'Harry, it's just a bit early for . . .'

'Where's my mother?'

'What?'

'I want my mother. Where is she?'

'Harry, don't . . .'

'Where is she?'

'She's . . . dead, Harry.'

He looked incredulously at her. As if he was waiting for the punch line, and then slowly the realization dawned and his shoulders started to shake, his head dropped, and he began to cry. Big, bone-shaker sobs.

Ruth didn't know what to do, where to look. She stood there, arms folded, knowing she was being cold and heartless, but knowing also why she was, why she couldn't move, why she couldn't hug or console him. She knew it looked bad, but nobody else knew what she knew. About life with Harry McKee, television star.

Ruth turned as the door behind her opened. Claire with her dirty blond hair and her sweet smile, and God dammit, her daddy's confidence. One fleeting glimpse, and she had the situation assessed and a decision made. Act like nothing was amiss. That there were no tears of despair. It was a chirpy, 'Hiya, Daddy!' and a kiss to her mother's cheek.

Harry looked up. *My* . . .?

He wiped the sleeve of his pyjamas across his face

as Claire beamed down at him. 'Howya doin'?' she asked.

'I . . .' He couldn't speak. She was absolutely beautiful. He looked disbelievingly from Claire to Ruth and back. His face was a sudden rainbow after a downpour.

'I brought this,' Claire said, showing him a white plastic bag. 'Your wedding album. Do you wanna look at it?'

He had no choice, of course. She was on the bed beside him in an instant, the book open, pointing, describing, reminiscing.

Ruth bit at her lip. All the things she should be doing.

She told them she was going to make a phone call. Claire smiled and gave her a little wink. Harry was already engrossed in the photographs. Ruth hadn't looked at them in years. There was no call to make. She just needed . . . distance. She stood outside the room and watched them through the glass. They were giggling.

Then the nurse who'd brought them tea was at her shoulder. 'How's he doing?' she said, nodding in at Harry.

Ruth took a deep breath. 'He's . . . God, I don't know. How would you feel if you couldn't remember the last twenty-five years of your life?'

'Relieved.' She gave Ruth a playful punch on the shoulder. 'C'mon, chin up. He'll be back to his old self in no time.'

She was already walking away when Ruth said, 'It's not his old self I want.'

13

Ms Boyle said it was in Ruth's best interests not only to have him walking but also talking in a reasonably sane manner. 'If he comes on like Mungo Jerry,' she argued, 'the magistrate might take pity on him and give him the house.'

So Ruth quickly settled into a routine of afternoon and evening visits. Claire came with her sometimes, but Billy refused point blank. She didn't force him.

Harry was always pleased to see her. When they talked, Ruth tried to steer the conversation back to their teenage years, so that they could have happy chats about experiences they'd shared. Harry, on the other hand, though being perfectly polite about it, was only interested in the missing years. She could understand that, but she was still under doctor's orders not to reveal to him what a shit he'd been or how big a star he'd become, and it was really starting to piss her off.

One day, he accused her of being vague. 'You're vague,' he said.

'I'm not vague.'

'Yes, you are, you're not telling me anything. The woman who serves the tea has told me more than you.'

Ruth grew suddenly anxious. 'What did she tell you?'

'Nothing. She's been sworn to secrecy as well.' He sighed. 'This is a bloody nightmare, nobody's telling me anything. Tell me the truth, Ruth. Is this some sort of secret government programme? Are they doing experiments on me? Has something gone drastically wrong? Am I in some weird parallel universe? It's something about time travel, isn't it? Is it about apes?'

'Apes?'

'Like *Planet of the Apes*. Have they taken over and we're in some sort of secure environment . . .'

'*Harry*. Stop it. Jesus. I'd forgotten how much into science fiction you were.' She rolled her eyes. 'There's *nothing* going on. You've lost your memory. I'm doing my best to fill in the blanks. I'm sorry if I'm *vague*.

It's just a big world out there. I don't know where
to start.'

Harry nodded thoughtfully. 'What about the
moon?'

'*What about* the moon?'

'Have you been there? The moon base?'

'No, Harry, there's no moon base.'

'What about Mars?'

'No, Harry.'

He tutted. 'Life on other . . .'

'No, Harry.'

'What about Elvis?'

'Now he *is* on the moon.'

'*Seriously?*'

'No. Sorry. A joke. Elvis is dead.'

'*Dead?*'

'Harry. Christ. Face it. If you remember nothing
after you were eighteen, and you're now into your
forties, one hell of a lot of people are going to be
dead. Nixon's dead! Sinatra! Steve McQueen! Jesus,
Harry, I could go on for ever. I can't remember
everything. Look, it's much better if you wait until
your memory comes back. Just be patient. It'll come
back.'

'Well, what if it doesn't?'

'Then . . . then . . .' She threw up her hands in
exasperation. 'It *will*.'

She brought him a big thick book called *Century – Almanac of a Hundred Years*, which broke the twentieth century down into a hundred chapters, with loads of pictures. It was aimed at kids and the educationally subnormal, and Harry qualified on both counts. It cost her £4.50 in Bargain Books. She brought him a five-CD set of *The Rock'n'Roll Years* she got for £7 in a Woolies bargain basket and borrowed Billy's Discman to play them on. On successive days she brought him a Pop-Tart, a Pot Noodle and a Mars Bar Ice Cream. She tried to explain the Internet, a palm-top computer and Nike Air Jordans. He was a sponge and she was . . . well, she didn't want to go there.

When he was confused or frustrated Harry got a face on him like a Lurgan spade. She tried hard to stop herself from laughing when she saw it. It was like talking to a little boy. Yet not. She thought suddenly of the *Jungle Book* and Man-Cub. That's what he was. Man-Cub, struggling to understand his place in the world.

'They want to send me home,' he said suddenly one afternoon.

'*What?*' A spike of panic shot through her. 'Have they said . . .?'

'No . . . they just keep coming round and staring at my bed. They think I'm faking, don't they?'

'No . . . not at all. There's a shortage of beds.'

'Have they stopped making them?'

'What?' She sighed. 'No. Look. It's just . . . do you *want* to go home?'

'I want to go *back.'*

There was nothing she could say to that.

Harry read anything he could lay his hands on. They brought him the newspapers each morning, but he always found that certain stories had been clipped out before they reached him, and he couldn't understand why. He asked, but the nurse waved him away, saying he should be happy getting them for nothing. He would have paid if he had any money, but Ruth hadn't brought him any. He kept reminding her, and she kept forgetting. It was only at the end of his third week in hospital that he discovered that there was a small library on the floor below.

Eventually, after much pestering, he was wheeled down.

He found an elderly, whiskered woman in a crocheted shawl sitting behind a desk, ready to sign books in and out, but business was obviously slack and she was too engrossed in her crocheting to even look up when Harry was wheeled in. He had been fingering his way along the cracked spines for five minutes when she said suddenly, 'I used to be chief librarian in Armagh. And now I'm reduced to this.'

Harry glanced back at her. 'Are you . . .?'

'Upstairs waiting for a kidney.'

Harry nodded. She was paying more attention to him now, moving in her seat for a better view. Harry concentrated on the books. They were mostly paperbacks in rather poor condition. One had a stamp inside that said it had been donated to the hospital in 1981. He wondered how many sick and dying hands each book had passed through, and whether the yellowed pages before him still contained some memory of that person, or worse, some evil germ or mutating cell. He imagined that every disease known to man was present in this tiny room, soaked into those flimsy pages, just waiting for an opportunity to burst forth in a deadly untreatable form that would wipe all human life from the face of . . .

'I love watching you.'

Harry glanced round again. 'Excuse me?' he said. She had come out from behind her desk. She was flattening her grey hair with one hand and smiling down at him.

'I said, I love watching you.'

'Oh.' He shrugged. 'Thank you.'

'My husband loves your buns.'

Harry began to lift books at random.

'Especially with icing sugar on them.'

It wasn't a kidney she needed, Harry decided, but electric shock treatment. In a few moments he had half a dozen books in his lap. Thrillers, chillers, authors and titles he didn't recognize. He didn't care, he wanted out. He couldn't handle senile old bats. His granny had gone like that. He wheeled himself across to her table. She quickly took her seat again and nodded at the books. 'You're keen,' she said, lifting them up one by one.

'Been away,' Harry said quickly, 'catching up.'

She nodded thoughtfully for a moment, then smiled at him a little self-consciously. 'I wonder . . . could I ask you something?'

Harry nodded slowly.

'I'm having terrible trouble with my dumplings.'

Harry's mouth dropped open.

'I was wondering if you had any advice.'

Harry was having difficulty finding the right words. 'I . . . well, I . . . the fact is . . . it's just . . . I need to go to the toilet.'

He grabbed the wheels and reversed quickly to the door. He smiled weakly at her, then aimed his wheelchair down the corridor and took off at speed.

'What about your books?' the librarian called after him.

He laughed with relief once he was a safe distance away. God, he thought, there aren't half some loonies on the loose.

The nurse who'd wheeled him down had given him strict instructions to stay in the library, and she would come back down and get him in twenty minutes, but that was still a quarter of an hour away. Besides, there was nothing wrong with him physically. He could just as easily get up and walk back to his room. But hospital policy was hospital policy.

Anyway, it was good fun free-wheeling down the corridor.

He rolled, and he rolled, and he rolled some more.

At one busy junction he jumped out of his chair and shouted, 'I can walk! I can walk! It's a miracle!' but he was studiously ignored.

Later he realized that he'd no idea where he was. At some point he must have crossed into a different building. The decor, the lay-out, the ambience was different. He rolled on. He had no intention of asking for directions. He rolled on. He didn't know *who* he was, what did it matter *where* he was? His mother was dead. Ruth was . . . *older*. Beautiful still. But not . . . Jesus, she'd only been a wee girl. They hadn't been going out that long. She had been warm and lively and loving, and now she was cold and . . . he searched for the right word. *Dormant*.

Eventually he found an elevator and reasoned that it would at least bring him back to the right level. He pressed the button. As he waited for it to arrive he became aware of a man standing beside him. Harry nodded up at him. The man said nothing, but stared back. Harry looked away. It was really annoying, everyone staring at him all the time. It wasn't his fault he'd lost his memory. He was sure there were more interesting cases in the hospital. Why'd they all have to stare at *him*? Harry continued to look straight ahead, but he could see in the reflection on the elevator doors that the man was still staring at him. Harry guessed he was maybe in his thirties, possibly forties. He was wearing a blue hospital gown. His neck was in a brace, his face was bruised and scraped. He was supporting himself on a three-legged metal frame, but there was definitely something about his demeanour that suggested his problem was more mental than physical.

Still no lift.

The man said, 'My life is in tatters.'

Harry, embarrassed, said, 'Sorry.'

'I've resigned my seat in the house.'

'That's . . . unfortunate.'

'My wife has left me. I'm a laughing stock.'

'Oh . . . dear.'

'And it's all your fault.'

This time Harry did look round, but only the zimmer frame remained. The man himself had moved behind him and was now holding onto Harry's chair for support. The elevator *pinged* and the doors slid open. Harry tried to move his chair forward, but couldn't. The man was holding it still.

'Let me,' said the man.

'No, it's okay, I can manage . . .'

But instead of moving him forwards, the man began to pull Harry's chair backwards. He swung it to the left and then pushed it and Harry through a set of swing doors.

Harry was doing his best to remain polite. 'Really . . . I'm not this way . . . upstairs . . .'

'It's all your fault, you fat bastard!' the man suddenly bellowed. Harry tried to get out of the chair, but they were going too fast now.

'Look . . . please . . . just . . . !'

Faster and faster and faster. They came to another set of doors, this time marked FIRE EXIT. The man giggled and slammed the chair through them and out into the open air.

Harry's eyes widened in terror. The man pulled

the wheelchair to a halt at the top of a steep flight of metal steps leading to a car park below.

'I think we should go . . .' Harry began, but the man suddenly gave the chair a good hard shove, pitching it over the edge and down the steps at considerable speed.

Harry tried to hang on, but the chair only stayed upright for the first half dozen steps, then toppled over, hurling him out into the afternoon air with a shout. He landed with a thump and then tumbled the rest of the way down to the ground.

He had a vague notion of someone laughing uproariously, then everything faded away to black.

14

Ruth took the call at home. She had half a dozen framed photographs under her arm. Claire was just coming through the front door. She hushed any greeting until the nurse had finished telling her about Harry's little accident. She thanked the nurse for letting her know, then put the phone down.

'Is Daddy . . .?' Claire asked anxiously.

'He's fine. He just took a bit of a tumble.'

Billy came into the hall, a similar collection of photographs in his arms. 'Proving my point exactly,' he said. 'He's a liability, a friggin' empty head.'

'He's your dad, Billy,' Ruth said, setting the photos

down in a cardboard box at the foot of the stairs. 'We have certain responsibilities.'

'He never had.'

'Well, that's what makes us wonderful human beings.'

Claire took her coat off and hung it up. She knelt beside the cardboard box. 'What're you doing?' she asked as she began to flick through the pictures.

'Destroying the past!' Billy trumpeted.

'We're not destroying anything,' Ruth said quickly. 'Just following doctor's orders. You know they said he wouldn't be able to handle the celebrity thing for a while, so this lot is going into storage.' She stood beside Claire and looked down at the pictures. Harry with Terry Wogan. Harry with Sacha Distel. Harry with Harry Secombe. Dozens of others. The one thing they all had in common was Harry, and the fact that Ruth wasn't in any of them.

Claire smiled round at her. 'You mean he's coming home?'

'They won't keep him in the hospital because there's nothing physically wrong with him. Even after his accident.'

'So we're lumbered with him,' said Billy.

Ruth tutted. 'Would you have him sleeping on the footpath?'

'I'd have him sleeping on the *road*.'

149

'C'mon, Billy,' said Claire, 'it's probably just until he's back on his feet.'

Ruth moved to the stairs and began to lift down the photos that lined the wall from bottom to top.

Billy stood scowling at Claire. 'That's easy for you to say. You don't have to live with him.' He looked accusingly at his mother. 'We had this all planned out. We were going to start enjoying ourselves again.'

Claire shook her head. 'Billy . . . *Billy* . . . don't you see that by helping Daddy in his time of crisis, we also help ourselves?'

'Yes, o philosopher, we want to help ourselves to the house, to the car and to as much child support as we can squeeze out of the bastard.'

'Billy!' Ruth snapped from halfway up the stairs. 'That's not nice.'

'It's a direct quote from you.'

Ruth rolled her eyes.

'Mum, you can't bring him home, you can't expect . . .' Billy stopped suddenly. His brow furrowed. 'Unless . . . *unless* . . . Mum?' His voice was suddenly alive with excitement. 'You *dark horse.*'

Ruth looked at him. *'What?'*

'It's the classic double bluff, isn't it?'

Ruth snorted. 'I don't know what you're talking

about.' She lifted another photo off its hook and blew the dust away.

'*He's* trying to fool *us*, but you want to bring him home so we can catch *him* . . . then he won't have a leg to stand on when it comes to court. *Mum*. I didn't think you could be so cold and calculating.'

Claire was looking at her oddly. 'Mum . . . you couldn't . . . you wouldn't . . . you used to love him.'

'*I* didn't,' said Billy.

Ruth looked from one to the other, then laughed. 'I've never heard anything so ridiculous.' She blew dust off the next photo, then handed the five under her arm to Billy. He handed them on to Claire and she placed them in the box with the others. Ruth came back down the stairs, brushing dust off her blouse. 'Look,' she said, 'there is no master plan, okay?' She ruffled her son's hair. 'Billy, if you want to try and catch him out, well, that's up to you, okay? Maybe he'll prove you wrong. All I'm saying is that we're still getting divorced, and all we're doing is helping him get back on his feet, okay?'

Billy nodded doubtfully. There was more than a hint of suspicion in Claire's eyes.

Ruth looked back along the hall, and then up the stairs. The wallpaper had once been white, but over the years it had gradually changed to a kind of nicotine yellow. Now there were more than a dozen clean white rectangular shapes along the walls where the photos had hung. They stuck out like sore thumbs.

Ruth was convinced that Harry wouldn't even notice.

15

Harry was released on a Saturday morning, even though there was an unwritten rule that patients didn't get sent home at weekends. It was supposed to be bad luck, but they made an exception for Harry. He had become quite a handful. Not in a bad way, Professor Simmington emphasized as they wheeled him down towards the car park. He kept his voice low, walking beside Ruth, while Harry chatted happily to the small group of nurses who'd taken it upon themselves to escort him out. Harry, the professor said, was just . . . disruptive. Excessive. Depressive. Irrepressible. Withdrawn. Motormouthed. Uncommunicative. Cheeky. Respectful. A child. A man. He was every opposite in the book, sometimes the book was hard, sometimes it was soft, sometimes it gave the impression of being well thumbed, sometimes it was fresh off the press.

Ruth had had her fill of Professor Simmington's allusions. She thought he could do with taking a couple of pills himself, just to slow him down. She wanted to say: *Harry's a pain in the hole, so you're sending him home to annoy me.*

When they got to the car park, one of the nurses asked Harry for an autograph. The professor looked at her like thunder, and she quickly flustered something about how she always got her best patients to sign her autograph book.

Ruth shook her head. *He doesn't know who the hell he is, but he's still signing autographs.*

When the nurses left, they took his wheelchair with them. As the professor gave her some final pieces of advice, Ruth glanced across at Harry, standing half a dozen yards away on the edge of the kerb, scanning the car park for the taxi they'd ordered. Claire had a long-standing arrangement to borrow the car for the day, but she was all for giving it up when she heard her daddy was getting out. Ruth wouldn't hear of it. Frankly, she would have made Harry walk home if there hadn't been so many people watching. He had one hand thrust into the pocket of his trousers, the other was raised to the lapel of his jacket, caressing the material. He looked rather forlorn. Crumpled, even. After a few moments the professor realized she was no longer listening, and followed her gaze.

'Nobody said it was going to be easy, Ruth,' he said quietly.

She nodded, then together they walked across to him. Simmington put a hand on Harry's shoulder and he turned slowly towards them. His face showed an odd mixture of anticipation and fear.

'This must be quite exciting for you, Harry,' said the professor.

'Yeah. Like going over the top at the Somme was exciting.' He glanced at Ruth, standing frowning, then back across the car park. 'Am I going to be okay, Professor?'

Simmington squeezed Harry's shoulder. 'Harry, in medicine there are no absolutes. We don't give promises. We give Prozac.'

Harry's brow furrowed. 'If I knew what that meant, I'm sure I'd find it funny.'

'You will, Harry, you will. I'm sure you'll be fine.' He winked. 'Come back and see us, Harry. Don't be a stranger.'

He shook hands with Ruth, then walked back into the hospital. Harry watched him go, then shook his head. 'What sort of stupid bloody comment was that?' he asked Ruth. *'Don't be a stranger.* Of course I'm a bloody stranger. Stranger in a strange land.'

'Harry, you're getting back on to science fiction.' Without thinking, she slipped a hand through his arm. 'C'mon. Here's the cab.'

She knew, deep down, that he wasn't faking. That he wasn't that good. That he was mediocre in everything he chose to do, whether it was cooking, presenting, interviewing or being a human being. To carry off this whole amnesia thing would have required Oscar-level talent, and he simply didn't have it. He *couldn't* be faking. She watched him fumble with the rear seat belt. Jump when the electronic window rolled down. Look startled when the device on the dash alerted the driver to a speed trap.

They were sitting as far apart as they could in the back seat, with Harry's face glued to the window, his eyes darting from shop to shop to shop.

Ruth jumped when something touched her hand, thinking it was an insect or a mouse or something, but it was Harry, taking her hand, squeezing it, holding on for support. She didn't quite know how to react. It had been so long. She sat there stiffly, her fingers hard and unwieldy, staring ahead.

'What's McDonald's?' Harry asked suddenly, his

head bent against the window, looking back. 'Is it a restaurant?'

'Debatable,' Ruth said.

The driver, watching Harry in the mirror, said: 'Been in hospital a long time, mate?'

'Twenty-five years,' Ruth replied tartly.

The driver's eyes flitted from her to Harry, and back to the road. 'Christ,' he said, 'I'd've asked for a second opinion.'

Ruth smiled weakly. There was silence for the next hundred yards or so, and Ruth thought that she might have got off lightly, but she thought it too soon.

'Do you know what I do when I'm feelin' poorly?' the driver asked. Then waited.

'No,' Ruth said eventually.

'Aromatherapy.' He let it sit in the air for a few moments. Then: 'One smell of that hospital and I run a fuckin' mile.'

He cackled.

Harry looked at Ruth. 'What's arom—'

'Later,' Ruth said quickly.

Another mile further on the driver started again. 'I had that Gerry Adams in the back the other day.' Harry mouthed *Gerry* . . .? at her, but Ruth quickly shook her head. 'Do you not think he's the dead spit of Rolf Harris?'

'"Two Little Boys",' said Harry quickly, glad of something familiar at last.

'Damn right they are,' replied the driver, 'and isn't it interesting you never see them in the one place at the same time?'

They drove down the broad sweep of road along the coast towards Donaghadee. The sun was shining brightly, the sea was calm, the Copeland Islands across the way seemed to glow. Harry stared contentedly out of the window. He was still holding her hand. She had removed it several times, on the pretence of scratching her nose or fixing her hair, but each time he had taken it back. After a while she'd just left it there.

Harry sat up suddenly as the taxi pulled into the driveway. He leaned forward for a closer look at the house, then turned puzzled, questioning eyes on Ruth. She nodded. A warm, excited smile appeared on his face. She couldn't help grinning in response. He *was* like a big kid.

He jumped out as soon as the car stopped, then stood staring up, his mouth hanging open.

Ruth lifted Harry's bag out, then paid the driver. She even gave him a tip, *Don't talk so much*, and a pound.

When the taxi finally pulled away, Harry turned

to her. 'Waaow!' he said. 'It's *incredible*.' She nodded. 'It must have cost a *fortune*.'

'It still does.'

She lifted his bag and walked ahead of him into the house.

He padded after her, like a puppy. He scampered into the hall, up the stairs, down the stairs, along the hall, into the kitchen, into the conservatory. He stared at the swimming pool filled with garbage. He ran back up the stairs and through the bedrooms, out onto the wide roof terrace they'd built over the double garage. He stared out at the Copelands and let out a *whoop*. He ran and he ran and he ran. Ruth was half scared that he'd have a heart attack. And half scared that he wouldn't. She busied herself with the dinner while Harry jogged around the garden, peering behind plants, over walls. He came inside and started going through the cupboards. Some of them were locked and he pulled at them, moved on, came back to them, pulled again. He didn't ask for a key. He nearly had a fit when he saw the size of the TV. She had to leave the dinner and come in and explain the video, the satellite and the DVD, then the remote controls that went with them. He flicked through the first three television channels, then flicked back again. She took the controls off him and moved on to Channel 4. His eyes widened. Then Channel 5. He mouthed, '*Five* channels?' She grinned and flicked on to 20, then 35, then 60, then 99.

'Holy God!' he exclaimed. 'A hundred channels!'

'Yeah. And some of them in English too. We'd be lost without them.'

He had the controls himself now, flicking, flicking, flicking. 'Cracker. It must be so educational.'

'Sure. Kids can now tell you to piss off in six different languages.'

She laughed and returned to the kitchen. He called after her: 'You didn't used to talk like that.'

I didn't used to be married to an arsehole.

'Sorry,' she said instead, 'times change. Do you want a cup of tea?'

'*Yes, please!*' He said it with the enthusiasm of an addict. She was just about to bring it in to him when she heard the theme to *What's Cookin'?* , and it froze her where she stood. *Shit*. She'd forgotten about the Saturday repeat of the best bits of the week's show. She heard the excited MC saying *with guest presenter, Michael Bay!* and the audience roaring its approval.

She forced herself out of the kitchen and into the lounge. Harry was standing staring at the screen as Michael Bay, the similarly plump, red-haired local chef who'd replaced him, ambled onto the screen.

'Good morning and welcome to the show,' he

said, his voice as soft as butter. 'Today – bored with beef, chilled out on chicken? We'll be talking to an ostrich farmer who doesn't keep his head buried in the sand . . .'

'I see local TV's as crap as ever,' Harry said, then flicked to the next channel. Ruth looked at him, searching for a hint of something – memory, embarrassment, guilt – but there was nothing, just that same excited glow. She almost said something herself, but then changed her mind. No, not yet. She hurried back into the kitchen.

Ten minutes later he was in the attic, rooting through boxes of his old clothes, fingering his way through his collection of long players, his books, his photo albums. Ruth had already been through them to weed out anything that might give away his occupation. She wasn't completely convinced that it was the right way to go about it, but the professor had been adamant. *Sudden exposure to his notoriety could set him back months, Ruth. The shock of it might send him into a tailspin from which he might never recover. You know the polar bears you see in the zoo, mindlessly pacing from wall to wall because . . .*

She'd timed out. Harry was due to go back to the hospital the following week so that progress could be assessed. The professor had warned her that his returning memory – presuming that it *did* return – would probably be selective. That he might remember certain things, but not be able to place them in the right context. He would be confused, vulnerable, in need of support and guidance. Ruth said she had a number for the Samaritans and he looked at her like *she* had a slate loose.

'How's memory lane?' Ruth shouted up the ladder to the attic.

'Dusty,' Harry called back. She turned away, but he immediately called after her. 'Wait there, I want to show you something. Close your eyes.'

'Harry . . .'

'Close them.'

She tutted, but closed them all the same. She heard oddly heavy footsteps cross the ceiling above her, then stepped back as Harry came down the ladder.

'No peeking,' he said.

'Just bloody hurry up, Harry, I haven't got all . . .'

'Keep them closed . . . there now. One, two, three . . . *open!*'

She opened.

'Holy fuck, Harry!' She burst into laughter.

He looked a little crestfallen.

'I'm sorry, Harry, but . . . *Jesus* . . .'

He was wearing an Afghan coat. Platform boots, purple. A huge pair of flares, tangerine. He'd an electric guitar in his hands. He looked absolutely ridiculous.

'I think it looks pretty cool.'

'No, Harry. Once, maybe. And maybe not even then.'

'I was wearing this lot when you met me.'

'Harry, please, don't remind me. It was a long time ago.'

'No, it wasn't,' he shot back. 'It was only a few months.'

She sighed. *God, Harry. Look at the state of you, you stupid big eejit.*

She was saved, after a fashion, by the front door opening, closing, and then rapid footsteps on the stairs.

'Mum!' Billy called on his way up. 'When's the Teletubby coming home?'

He stopped dead at the top of the stairs. Ruth obligingly stepped to one side so that he could get a full and proper look at his father in all his glory.

She expected that he would laugh, and take the mickey, but instead a look of utter contempt appeared on his face.

'Oh, ho-ly shite,' said Billy.

Ruth glanced at Harry. *His* look couldn't have been more different. She realized suddenly that this was the first time he'd actually set eyes on his son in the flesh. Billy had refused to go to the hospital all along.

'Billy . . .?' Harry murmured. He set the guitar down carefully. He took a step towards his son, getting ready for a hug, but Billy, his lip curled in disgust, turned away and walked calmly back down the stairs.

'Billy!' Ruth shouted after him, but he just kept walking. She turned to Harry and started to apologize, but he shushed her.

'There's plenty of time,' he said.

No, there's not, Harry.

16

Harry watched *Robot Wars* and then *Pokemon*. When Ruth called him through for dinner Billy was already sitting at the kitchen table. He cast a contempt-filled glance at his dad, then concentrated on staring at the table. Harry, conversely, couldn't take his eyes off him. His son. *My son. A* fine-looking fella. He wanted to talk to him about music and football and television and . . .

'See enough?' Billy snapped.

'You see enough?' Harry snapped back.

'*You* were lookin' at *me*!'

'You were lookin' back. Anyway, see ya, wouldn't wanna be ya.'

'Oh, grow up.'

'Yeah . . .' Harry fumbled about for ammunition. 'At least . . . I'm not a dwarf.'

'I'm thirteen. I'll grow. And presumably not backwards, like some people I could mention . . .'

Ruth hurried across from the counter. 'Boys . . . *boys* . . .' she scolded, setting a plate before each of them. 'That's enough . . . c'mon.'

She returned for the salad bowl. Billy stared at his plate. 'What is this crap?'

Ruth smiled. 'What's it look like?'

'It looks like a baked potato and a kwish.'

'*Quiche*,' corrected Harry.

'I know what it is,' snapped Billy. 'Why are we eating kwish?'

'*Quiche*,' said Harry.

'Because,' said Ruth, finally sitting down, 'you know your father has been watching his weight.' She was trying to catch Billy's eye, so she could wink at him, get him to play along like they'd agreed, but he was lost in a flush of insolence and wouldn't meet her eye. 'This is his favourite.'

'*What?*' said Billy, finally looking up. Before she could respond he'd pushed his plate away. 'I'm not eating this shite. And youse are both off your heads.'

He stood, his chair screeching on the linoleum, then stalked out of the kitchen.

'Billy!' Ruth shouted after him, but he was away.

'Do you want me to . . .?' Harry began, but he stopped as soon as he saw the stern look on Ruth's face. He nodded. 'Maybe it's a bit soon.'

She sighed. 'I'm sorry,' she said, 'he's just at that age.'

Harry nodded. He gave a little laugh. 'I suppose I am as well.'

She smiled weakly.

They ate in silence for a while, until the sound of drumming came from upstairs.

'He's very good,' Harry said, rolling his eyes up to the ceiling.

'No, he's not, he's awful.'

They both nodded, and that broke the ice. They started talking. She still felt awkward. She was angry at Billy, but also quite envious. She was jealous of his freedom to shout at Harry, to rant, to throw the kwish in his face and tell him what a shit he'd been. But here she was, the perfect host, trying to make small talk over health food.

Harry had, THANK GOD, changed out of his seventies duds. He was wearing black canvas trousers and a red sweater. He'd had a bath, combed his hair, he was looking smarter than she'd seen him in a long time. He was eating quite happily. In the past he would have disappeared as fast as Billy if she'd put a quiche in front of him. She tried to remember the

167

last time they'd sat and eaten a meal together, just the two of them, but she couldn't. Now here they were. He, keen as mustard, full of questions, but still awkward, anxious not to make a fool of himself; she just anxious, her stomach in knots.

'What's typical then?' he asked.

He wanted to know about his life, *their* life. She'd started lying to him in the hospital when he'd asked about the drink, now she couldn't help but continue it. In a strange way, as she talked, fabricated, she found herself quite enjoying it, indulging in a little fantasy, an idealistic picture of how their life might have been if he hadn't turned into a monster.

What did it matter that none of it was true?

She didn't love him, they were getting divorced, he would be out of her life for ever.

'Oh, we set the alarm for seven, but you get up first. You bring me a cup of tea in bed. Then we go out for a jog.' He was nodding enthusiastically. 'Then a nice breakfast. You know, muesli, lots of fruit. You love fruit. Then you go off to work . . .'

'Political reporter, eh?'

'Y-yeah.'

'God, everything's changed. All I remember is the bombs and the soldiers and everyone hated each other. And now we all seem to love each other.'

'I wouldn't go that far. Anyway, then after work . . .

well, we go out. We go out all the time. The pictures.
The theatre. Nice meal. Weekends away.'

'It sounds lush.'

'I suppose it was.'

'So how come I feel so . . . baggy?'

'We're just getting older, Harry.'

He nodded thoughtfully, then munched silently
for the next few minutes. When he'd finished he
neatly arranged the knife and fork on his empty
plate, first one way, then the other, then back. Finally
satisfied, he looked up at her bemused face and asked:
'Do you love me?'

She tried to stop the colour rushing to her cheeks.
She tried not to avert her eyes. But she was helpless.
She looked away, she laughed, she dabbed her napkin
against her lips. 'What?'

'I said, do – you – love – me?'

She rearranged her own cutlery. She looked up at
him. 'You're my husband, Harry.'

'That's not what I asked.'

'Well, why wouldn't I?'

'And that's answering a question with a question,
and it's one I can't answer.'

Ruth blew air out of her cheeks. She stood
suddenly and lifted her plate. 'Love is . . . helping
with the dishes.'

She scurried over to the sink, her face burning.

A moment later he was behind her. 'Ruth, I . . .'

She moved sideways, like a crab. 'I'll get Billy to give you a hand with the dishes. He shouldn't get away with talking to us like that.'

Ruth was out in the hall and moving with speed. She shot up the stairs, heart pounding. *God, why can't I just tell him the truth?*

Because his memory will return soon enough.

Because you don't want him going into that tailspin.

Because that would threaten the divorce.

Because it would destroy him.

Because you're gutless.

She burst into Billy's room. He stopped battering the skins immediately. He looked meekly up at her. 'I'm sorry,' he started, 'I know . . .'

She held up a finger. He stopped. He knew her angry look too well. 'Go downstairs and help him with the dishes.'

'Mum . . .'

'Do it!' she snapped. He was out from behind the kit in an instant. He glared at her as he went past. 'I need your help on this, Billy.'

Ruth retired to her room. She lay down on her bed. This was Day One of Harry's return home and her head was spinning with the effort of it. What had she been thinking of? Why did she let people ride roughshod over her? Why had she listened to that Professor? Why did she listen to Ms Boyle? She should have said no, no, no. *He can rot in hospital. He's not my responsibility.* She rubbed her fists into her eyes. She massaged her scalp. It wasn't even like having the Harry she knew as a teenager home. That would have been different, easier. This was like having the old Harry, but stupid with it. Like he'd had a stroke or something, bumbling around like . . .

Oh, God, why am I so cruel?

'CLEAN!'

Ruth sat up in bed.

'CLEAN!'

Harry bellowing from downstairs.

'CLEAN!'

Ruth hurried out of her bedroom and down the stairs. Billy was standing outside the kitchen door, nearly doubled up with laughter. 'What's going on?' she hissed at him.

'CLEAN! CLEAN!'

Billy steadied himself against the wall. 'I . . . told him . . . the dishwasher was voice activated.'

'CLEAN!'

Ruth nearly laughed herself, but just managed to hold it in check. She pulled Billy off the wall and pushed him into the lounge. She held up the warning finger again. 'Billy, for God's sake! Honestly, you're a bad wee bugger at times.'

'CLEAN!'

She rolled her eyes. 'If you want to try and catch him out, that's up to you. But no filling his head with crap. Okay?'

'Okay,' Billy said weakly.

'FRIDGE-OPEN!'

Ruth looked at her son, and they both laughed. She sucked her cheeks in, tried to look serious, then turned for the kitchen.

'What used to hang here?' Harry asked later.

It was past eleven. Billy was long ago in bed. Ruth had tried to stop herself yawning in front of him, but it had been a long, stressful day, and still was. They were approaching the moment of truth. Dread hung upon her as a cold sweat.

Bed.

Or *BED!*

They stood in what had once merely been Harry's study, but which for the past few years had doubled as his bedroom. Ruth's was next door. She could tell *BED!* was on his mind as well. He had been hovering for ages, shifting his weight from foot to foot with the awkwardness and fidgety shyness of a virginal teenager, waiting for her to make the first move. Or was it because he was repelled by her and didn't know how to tell her? He was eighteen in his own head, how must he feel looking at her? Would he only be able to see crow's feet and wrinkles and cobwebs? Or would he be turned on by it? The older woman? Would he be thinking: *Mrs Robinson*?

What does it matter? Put the poor empty head out of his misery.

'I said, what used to hang here?'

She shook herself. He was looking at the spaces on the walls where his celebrity photographs had hung. 'Oh . . . just stuff. We had a clear-out a while back. We were going to redecorate.'

She smiled at him.

He said, 'I was wondering . . . ahm . . . it's getting late. And . . .'

'Oh! Sorry. *Of course*. Bed time!' He nodded enthusiastically. 'I . . . well, Harry.' She moved towards him and he stood ready to receive her, but she swerved past to stand by the settee behind him. She patted the arm of it. 'I hope you don't mind . . . more restful . . . just until things get back on a more even keel.' She bent into the settee, then pulled out the bed from within. She had a moment of panic about the sheets being stained and bloody from the night Harry was beaten up, but they were clean, and she remembered that Claire had changed them for

her. She straightened them and then turned nervously. 'Okay?' she said.

'Yes. Of course. Sure.' He tried to give it as much
enthusiasm as he gave everything these days, but
she could tell he was a little taken aback. It only
confirmed her belief that he wasn't that good an
actor. 'No problem,' he added.

She gave him a peck on the cheek goodnight, then
hurried out of the room. She closed the door behind
her and let out a little sigh of relief.

She was halfway down the stairs when she
thought: *Damn! Pyjamas!* She hurried to the hot press,
hunted out a pair, then returned to his room. She
knocked gently on the door.

If he heard, there was no response. She opened
the door. He was sitting on the very edge of the bed,
his face grim, his arms wrapped around himself, eyes
closed, gently rocking.

God.

She gave a little cough, and he jumped. In an
instant the happy-smiley face was back. He stood
up. 'Hiya,' he said.

'PJs,' she said quickly.

'Of course. Great. Yeah.'

He hurried across and took them off her.

'Night, then,' she said.

'Night.'

'I'm just . . . next door if you want anything.'

'Okay, great.'

She backed out of the room, nodding and smiling like a loon. She closed the door after her and thought immediately: *Christ, did that sound like an invitation?*

An hour later, in complete darkness, there was a tap on the dividing wall. It was only a plasterboard effort, and she knew from the ghastly past experience of a hundred screaming rows that the sound travelled through it like it wasn't there.

She was wide awake. Hadn't been able to get over. Hadn't been able to switch off.

Her first thought was: *He's coming in, he's going to get all romantic, Christ.*

'Ruth? Are you awake?'

'Y-yes, Harry.'

'I just wanted to say, I'm sorry.'

She sat up. 'What for?'

'I don't know.'

'Well, that makes sense.'

'I know. I . . . ahm . . . I'll see you in the morning.'

'Okay, Harry.'

And then silence. She lay back. What was he on about? Had he remembered something? Was that it? Or was *she* so bad at the acting that it was bleeding obvious that she was playing him for a fool? Should she go in to him, explain? Justify?

No.

Not justify, condemn. Condemn him for ruining everything. She should bloody well just throw him out, right here, right now. Drag him out of bed and push him down the stairs. Kick him when he reached the bottom and say, *There, that's for all the shit you've given me over the years.*

She sighed. *If only.*

Take a deep breath.

Relax.

Sleep. Start fresh in the morning.

Of course, she was awake until dawn.

17

She lies in a half-awake state, like Nebraska.

She is back at the wedding, dancing to 'Coz I Luv You' by Slade. The spotlights are on them in the middle of the dance floor, everyone is clapping. Can she be any happier?

So where did it all go wrong?

She remembers reading about Aids, and the spread of the HIV virus, and how some scientist or other had been able to track the first case back to some village in Africa in the 1920s. Can she do that, can she pick out the exact day where it all started to go pear-shaped, when Harry began his journey from loving husband to . . . virus?

There was a night when Claire was a toddler and

Billy was just a few weeks old. Claire was covered in chicken-pox and wearing little gloves to stop her scratching, but she was screaming the place down anyway. Then Billy was screaming as well and it just seemed to go on and on. She was still weak from the birth, she needed help, she needed Harry. Where was he? He was out at some club. She called him there, asked him to come home, but he said he couldn't, he was working, he had to check out an act for the show, it was part of his job, but she needed him there and then, not later, drunk, and she screamed at him and he screamed back about her not understanding his work and not taking him seriously.

Was that it, Ruth, was that when it started, when you realized you were alone?

Or was it before that again?

Was it when he came home from that interview with Frankie Woods, and he wanted nothing to do with a bloody cooking job on a crap variety show? Who was it who persuaded him to take it? He was into politics, into serious journalism, but you had one eye on the bigger house, the bigger car. You accused him of being an idealist, of not thinking of his family, you talked about the difference the money would make, couldn't he see that? Obligingly Claire started to cry. It was January, money was tight . . . but Christ, it was hardly

Angela's Ashes, was it? He had a good job, a good
wage . . .

You were greedy, Ruth.

He didn't want the job, but you did.

You pushed him into it.

You corrupted him.

You wanted the money, and then to meet famous
people. You encouraged him to attend parties, to
drink; you loved it.

Then you changed your mind, and you expected
him to change with you. But it was too late.

It was your fault.

Your fault.

Your . . .

She sat up suddenly in bed. She had sweated through
her pyjamas. She shook herself. Mad crazy dreams.
*Of course it wasn't my fault No one forced him to sleep
with half the women in Ireland.*

Ruth rolled out of bed. She glanced at the bedside
clock. It was a little after ten. Christ, she'd slept in.
Still, it was a Sunday morning. She could do what she
wanted. The front door slammed. Ruth padded across
to the window. Harry and Billy were walking together
down the drive. She smiled. Evidently they were getting
on a bit better. She knew Billy would be okay with
him after a while. Sure wasn't Harry a big kid too?

She took a long, relaxing shower, dressed, then went down for breakfast. She was halfway through her Alpen when she spotted the note. It was folded on the kitchen counter. It could have been anything. She might just as easily have ignored it. She opened it up.

Taken Fat Boy Swimming.

'Fuck!'

Ruth threw her plate in the sink, grabbed her keys and ran for the car.

The stupid boy, the stupid, stupid boy. What was he thinking of?

She almost crashed the car, twice – once as she came out of the drive and once at the traffic lights opposite the pool. She screamed to a halt outside, left the engine running on double yellow lines, then raced through the doors, bunking the queue and ignoring the girl hammering on the window of the ticket office. 'It's an emergency!' Ruth shouted back.

She took the stairs three at a time, ran through the ladies' changing room, dodged on tiptoes through the little rinse-off shower before finally emerging poolside. She quickly scanned the pool. Children right, adult left, diving pool straight ahead. She spotted Billy on the other side of the adult pool, just about to dive in. She shouted his name and he froze like a rabbit caught in headlights.

Ruth hurried round to him. 'Billy – you bad wee bugger!'

'What?' He was playing the innocent, but the guilt was tripping off him.

'What are you playing at? You know your father can't swim.'

He shrugged. 'Yeah. But does he?'

'Billy . . . where is he?'

'Still in the changing rooms I think.'

She gave a little sigh of relief.

And then: 'BILLLLLLLLLLLY!'

There he was, Harry McKee, not the smallest man in the world, running and jumping off the top diving board, plummeting into the deep pool like a meteor.

'Oh, Jesus Christ!'

A tidal wave came up and over the side of the diving pool. Billy laughed, but it drained away quickly, like he hadn't expected Harry to make quite such a splash of things.

His father surfaced. Briefly. He tried to yell something, but got a mouthful of water then went down again.

He came back up, arms flailing, then disappeared.

Ruth kicked off her shoes, pulled off her sweater,

then dived in, even as the pool attendants came running.

In the end it took six of them to get him out. Then he was on his side on the edge of the pool and choking up the chlorinated water while the soaked attendants stood around wondering whether it would be bad form to ask for an autograph just yet. One of them went and got Ruth a blanket.

Harry rolled onto his back. He was *smiling*. She couldn't believe the stupid bugger was smiling.

'That was *fantastic*,' he whispered, between coughs.

'Well, I'm glad you thought so,' Ruth snapped.

'Is it okay if I go for my swim now?' Billy asked.

Ruth angrily pointed the finger. 'You go and get changed this minute. And take your bloody father with you.'

Billy shrugged. Water off a duck's back. He walked off towards the changing rooms without waiting. One of the attendants helped Harry up. 'Are you okay, Harry?' he asked.

Harry nodded.

'My granny loves you.'

'Do I know her?' Harry asked, confused. 'Sorry, y'see I've lost . . .'

'No, of course you don't. She knows you though.' He smiled. 'Loves your wee cakes.'

Harry nodded, as if the penny had dropped, then turned puzzled eyes on Ruth. She shivered.

'Are you all right, Missus?' one of the other attendants asked.

'Do I look bloody all right?'

They walked out to the car fifteen minutes later, Ruth in a borrowed white T-shirt and a pair of manky tracksuit bottoms.

Harry skipped along beside her, full of the joys of spring. 'That was *great* . . .'

'Just get in the car.'

'Mum . . .' Billy began.

'And you just wait until I get you home.'

'Now come on,' Harry said, as Ruth stood with the door open, 'it's no one's fault I can't remember what I've forgotten.'

He climbed in. Ruth glared across at her son.

'His life didn't pass in front of him, then?' Billy asked.

'No, but yours will,' Ruth promised as he climbed in the other side.

18

Ruth tried hard to be really annoyed by Harry's constant enthusiasm, his smile and his laugh, his running commentary and incessant questioning, but gradually, gradually, day by day, it became more difficult.

The truth was that she found it such a pleasant change that she was actually half enjoying his company. He could be funny when he tried, he could be considerate, he could even listen, which he hadn't done for years.

She had to keep reminding herself: *he's a shit, he's a shit, he's a shit. This is a false dawn, he's a booby trap waiting to explode in my face.* And then she would step back, grow cold, become distant, and Harry would be left puzzled and hurt.

Tough.

Get used to it.

It's a big bad world out there, Harry McKee.

Frankie Woods phoned to see how he was. Ruth played it cool. She disliked Frankie intensely, blamed him for leading Harry astray. The parties, the women – and for all she knew, the drugs – they could all be traced back to Frankie. He had wanted to manufacture a celebrity, but he had created a monster.

Ruth knew from the papers about the hundreds of letters the Broadcasting Complaints Commission had received about Harry's final, memorable performance on *What's Cookin'?* The Commission had exonerated Harry, due to his undiagnosed medical condition, and wished him a speedy recovery; it reserved its venom for Frankie, criticizing him in the harshest possible terms both for allowing the show to continue broadcasting live when Harry obviously wasn't well, and for the foul language he'd used on air, accidentally or not.

The Commission didn't have any powers to fine him or even fire him, but it did have influence with both broadcasters and advertisers, so it had been a shaky few weeks for Frankie. His production company's contract for *What's Cookin'?* was up for renewal at the end of the year, and things were not looking good. If guest presenter Michael Bay had been up to scratch, it might have helped, but he was, everyone agreed, a bit of a disaster. Oh, he could read the autocue just fine and he could expertly describe how to cook a perfect meal. But he had the personality of a damp piece of plywood, the charm of a bread pudding. Harry's material had always been poor but at least he'd been able to deliver it; Michael Bay lacked not just a funny bone, but a single funny cell.

So Frankie was crawling.

'You didn't come to see him in hospital, Frankie.'

'No . . . thought it better to . . . not.'

'You swore you would never work with him again. You swore quite a lot, from what I recall.'

'I was angry. I didn't understand he was sick. Forgive and forget, Ruth.'

'Well, he's certainly forgotten.'

'Yes, I . . . Will I come and see him?'

'No, it's too early.'

'Maybe if he saw me he might . . .'

'No, Frankie.'

'Okay. Okay. But as soon as there's any sign . . .'

'You bet.'

They made the occasional foray from the house. Ruth found that Harry went largely unnoticed if she kept him away from places where large numbers of elderly people congregated. She avoided shopping malls and coffee shops and concentrated on places with lots of steps. Video stores, computer games outlets, Internet cafes, these were the places where he was relatively safe from recognition. As an added precaution she got him to wear a baseball cap, and sometimes an anorak with the hood up, even when it wasn't raining. He was happy to do whatever she said. He never complained. He never picked a fight. He didn't express an interest in alcohol or fatty foods. After the first night, he never once questioned that he should sleep in his study. Sometimes she wished she knew what was going on in his head. Sometimes she thought there was probably too much going on in there, and other times not enough. He was an enigma. She wondered what would happen if his memory did come back – would he jump for joy, or would he not even tell her?

One morning Ruth was still sound asleep when heavy drumming suddenly erupted. She flew out of the bed in a rage. She'd warned Billy about it several times already, convinced that he was getting up earlier and earlier each morning just so that he could annoy his father by creating a God-awful racket. She stormed along the hall, yelling above the steady beat. 'Billy! I TOLD YOU YOUR DAD NEEDS PEACE AND' – she banged the door open – 'QUIET!'

She stopped dead.

Harry was behind the drums. He finished on a roll, then smiled across. 'Epic,' he said.

Before Ruth could say anything Billy barged past her and ripped the drumsticks out of Harry's hands. 'Just bloody leave them alone,' he said.

'I only wanted a wee go.'

'Well, they're mine, okay?'

'I wasn't doing any harm.'

'Aye, that's right, you never do.'

He spun on his heel and left the room. Harry watched him go, then drummed his fingers sheepishly on the snare.

'I'm going for a quick shower,' Ruth said, and left him to it.

Like having two bloody kids in the house.

While she lost herself for a few minutes in the hot water, Harry went downstairs. The post was just coming through the door. He picked the two letters up off the mat and examined them. There was one for Ruth, and one for him. He carried them into the kitchen, then set them on the counter. He lifted two eggs from the fridge and placed them in egg cups. Then he put them in the microwave. He closed the door and set the timer for four minutes. He filled the kettle. As he waited for the eggs to cook he picked up his letter. As he tore it open he fantasized idly on its contents. 'Dear Mr McKee,' he announced to the kitchen, to the whirring eggs and the spice rack and the mug tree, 'we are very pleased to tell you that we have located your missing memory. It was found by one of our nurses hiding in a cardboard box in the linen room . . .' He unfolded the letter and scanned the first few lines. Immediately he said, 'Oh.'

He read it, and he re-read it. He was damp with sweat. His legs felt shaky. He heard Ruth on the stairs and hurriedly stuffed the letter into his pocket.

She came through the door, still tying her dressing gown. 'Anything in the post?' she asked as she passed and his hand shot down to the counter. He lifted her envelope and handed it to her.

She peered at it for a millisecond. '*Reader's Digest*. They want to give me a million pounds.' She tutted. She crumpled the letter unopened and tossed it at the bin. 'Money would spoil us.' It bounced off the rim and landed on the floor. As Ruth turned from the cupboard with her cereal bowl she smiled as she saw Harry pick the envelope off the floor and place it carefully in the bin.

Haven't times . . .

BANG!

Ruth jumped, hand on heart, as the eggs in the microwave exploded.

'Jesus Christ, Harry!'

19

She left him to clean the microwave. She had an appointment with her solicitor, although she told him she was going to the dentist. 'Just a check-up,' she said. 'You're sure you'll be okay?'

'I'll be fine. Me and the control remote.'

Billy rolled his eyes and went on out to the car. He was going to football. He played for the Boys' Brigade, even though there wasn't a religious bone in his body.

'There's plenty in the fridge.'

'I will have a Healthy Options Chicken Tikka Masala and a Petit Filou.'

She hesitated, then gave him a peck on the cheek. 'I won't be long. Be careful.'

He nodded and waved them off.

As they headed out on the coast road towards Bangor, Ruth said, 'I thought I told you to stop filling his head with crap.'

Billy pulled his martyr face. 'What have I done now?'

'David Bowie is not the Chancellor of the Exchequer. Microsoft is not a small jelly-like substance used in playschool. And even he isn't stupid enough to believe that we can communicate by ESP.'

'I'm only winding him up.'

'Well, stop it. It's not fair.'

'You've changed your tune.'

'I have not. But at least I don't kick a man when he's down.'

'That's *exactly* when you should kick him. In fact, given the choice, I'd *shoot* him. Put him out of his misery.'

'Beg your pardon, Billy, but you seem to be the only one who's miserable around here.'

She was trying to concentrate on the traffic, but the briefest glimpse to her left was enough to confirm the incredulous look on his face.

'You're softening,' said Billy.

'I am not.'

'Yes, you are. You're starting to like him again. I can't believe you'd fall for it.'

'Fall for what?'

'The big act. For God's sake, Mum, open your eyes and listen to the roses.'

'It's *smell* the roses.'

'Yeah, well, they smell like bullshit to me.'

'Watch the language.'

'Yeah, I'd a good teacher.'

She dropped him off at the church in Bangor, then drove on to Belfast and Ms Boyle's immaculate office. It was only supposed to be a twenty-minute appointment, but Boyle wanted to know everything. When it hit thirty minutes Ruth suspected that she was dragging it out on purpose so that she could charge double, and aim for triple. When Boyle spotted Ruth glancing at the clock on the wall she laughed suddenly. 'Don't worry, Ruth, this one's on me. This is *fascinating*. You're absolutely certain there's no evidence of fakery?'

'No . . . he just sits there all day going, *this is new, how does this work? Rock Hudson was* gay?'

'But you've been watching him closely? You've marked the bottles of alcohol in case . . .?'

'There's no need, he just sits there going, *how do they do that? When did they discover that? Elton John's* gay?' She sighed. 'He's just so eager. How can anyone be that keen? It's like . . . it's like we're the ones with the problem . . .'

Ms Boyle was standing now, her hands clasped behind her like a Nazi. 'He's acting, Ruth, *acting.*' It sounded like *Achtung*! 'You have to remember that. Don't let him get to you. You just have to hang in there, continue to bring him along . . . it's important that he appears normal, that he can hold a coherent conversation. The magistrate *must be* convinced.'

Ruth emerged from her solicitor's office filled with new resolve. Ms Boyle was right. Whether he was faking or not, he was still the Harry McKee who'd ruined her life, she had to think of her own future happiness, and Billy's. Be strong.

She checked her watch. She had an hour to kill before she was due to pick Billy up again. Only one thing for it. Retail therapy.

As Ruth disappeared into clothes heaven, Harry climbed out of a taxi and stood nervously surveying Belfast city centre.

He remembered a dark, violent place, with security gates and body searches at every street corner. Bombs and bullets and murder and mayhem. When you couldn't enter a shop without raising your hands to be frisked. A ghost town at night, and a permanent nervousness by day.

Now music and brightness and money assailed him from all sides. It was like being in London! It was buy, buy, buy, and it wasn't even Christmas. It was hustle, bustle and Porsches parked on every corner. He would have liked to have walked and explored and experienced this brave new world, but he had urgent business.

He took the letter out of his pocket and examined the address again. He recognized the name of the street, but not the street itself. Everything had changed. Where there had once been crumbling mills and bombed-out pubs, there were now soaring skyscrapers and glistening hotels. He counted along, looking for the offices of JJ McMahon & Co, Solicitors. He found them eventually, the name one of more than a dozen on a small brass plate outside an impressive glass-fronted building. They wouldn't have dared build anything glass-fronted in his day, it would have been like a red rag to a bull. Wouldn't have lasted a week.

He was confronted with more glass when he went inside. A glass-fronted lift, but he didn't like the look of it, so took the stairs to the seventh floor. He was puffing and blowing a bit when he knocked and entered the solicitor's offices. In front of him a pigtailed receptionist sat with her feet on her desk, reading a magazine, chewing gum. It was several moments before she looked up, but when she did her bored expression quickly melted away.

'I'd like to see . . .'

'Harry! How're ya doin'? You're lookin' great.'

'I wonder if I could . . .'

'Oh, go on through.' She thumbed at a door behind her. Harry nodded and approached it, he raised his hand to knock, then glanced hesitantly back at the girl. 'Go on in,' she said, 'he's about as busy as I am.' She winked.

Harry knocked, then opened the door.

The man behind the desk was reading a magazine as well. He looked up with the same bored expression. 'Sorry, I . . . *Harry*?' JJ stood, smiling widely. 'Good God! Harry! How are you, old son?'

'Bewildered on all fronts, thank you.'

Harry shook hands with him, then sat glumly on a straight-backed chair.

'You look *wonderful* . . . how's the old amateur dramatics coming along?'

Harry ignored the question, and instead thrust the letter across the desk. 'What is this?' he asked.

Surprised, JJ glanced down. His brow furrowed. He picked it up. He looked at Harry. 'Harry . . . well, it's what it says. Are you sure you're feeling . . .?'

'Why would I want to get divorced?'

JJ gazed uncertainly at him for several moments, then broke into a smile again. 'Wonderful. It's like that method acting, isn't it? Give it one hundred per cent, you get one hundred per cent back . . .'

Harry brought his fist down on the table, hard, and JJ jumped. 'Just tell me what's going on!'

'Jesus!' JJ looked at Harry with sudden realization. 'Oh, my dear God, Harry . . . what did they do to you in that place?'

'What?'

'Things were going along quite nicely . . . Jesus, Harry, you didn't let them . . . electrodes' – he touched his skull – 'here and here . . . pulses of electricity . . . Did they boil your brain, Harry, did they?'

'Calm down.'

JJ was breathing hard. He pulled open a drawer and produced a bottle of Bushmills and two glasses. 'We both need a shot of this,' he said, and began to pour.

'I don't drink, Mr McMahon.'

'Oh, my God! They really did it!'

Harry thumped the table again. 'Will you listen to me? I was beaten up! I lost my memory! Now tell me about this divorce!'

JJ slumped back in his chair. 'Easy now, Harry . . . settle. Oh, goodness. This is a dreadful shock.' They looked at each other suspiciously for several moments. Then a last gasp of a twinkle appeared in JJ's eyes and he leaned forward again, smiling. 'Are you just winding me up?'

'Tell me!'

JJ shot backwards. 'Amnesia! My goodness! Harry, dear boy, it's really . . .' He took a deep breath. 'Harry, I'm afraid she rather has you over a barrel, as simple as that. We've been friends for twenty years, I can't be more blunt than that.'

'If we've been friends for twenty years, yes, you can.'

'Okay. Okay, Harry, have it your way. I thought we could run with this amnesia thing, maybe save the house . . .'

'I don't understand.'

JJ turned and lifted the stack of newspapers that sat permanently on the floor to the side of his desk. He set them on the table and slapped his hand down on the top one. 'Newspapers, Harry, newspapers.' He shook his head. 'Harry, if you really can't remember – well, then, you're the only one in the country doesn't know what a shit you've been.'

'What?'

JJ pushed the stack of papers across the table towards Harry, who immediately picked one up. 'Newspapers, Harry . . . every infidelity, every arrest – you have a genius for bad publicity.'

'But why would they be interested in me?' He

lifted a second, a third, a fourth. Fuzzy photos of him with dizzy blondes, snatched pictures of him lying asleep under a table, entering a courthouse, his face bruised, raising a hand to the camera. 'I don't understand.' He sighed, and it seemed to come from as far down as his feet. He felt weak. His hands gripped the edge of JJ's desk, his knuckles white, his face whiter. 'I don't . . . why would I? But I love *Ruth.*'

JJ raised his eyebrows, and spoke from experience. 'What's love got to do with it?' He let it sit in the air for a moment. 'I'm really sorry that it turned out this way, but I can only do so much.' He clinked his glass against the whiskey bottle. 'Are you sure you won't . . .?'

Harry shook his head. This was so much worse than he had feared. He was in despair. He wanted the ground to open up.

JJ sipped his drink. He blew air out of his cheeks. He had never seen his old friend so diminished. Not even when he was in his coma. He *had* gone to see him. He would wait until Ruth had finished her daily visit, then sneak in. He wouldn't say anything, just sit there and read the paper and sip from his flask of whiskey and think about old times.

Now Harry, his old friend, really did need him.

'Harry,' he began, 'I don't know much about

medicine, but it strikes me that you've got something a lot of us would like to have. The chance to start again.'

Harry looked up, desperate for inspiration.

'Do you know in a tumble dryer, there's a filter which gathers all the fluff that comes off your clothes? Well, God has cleaned your filter, Harry.'

Harry shook his head sadly. 'I don't even remember you.'

'Yeah, well, I made a bollocks of my life as well.' He lifted the letter he'd sent to Harry and examined it again. 'The new date for your divorce is the twenty-third. That's two weeks, Harry. Unless we can find some way of bringing her round, you'll be homeless, childless *and* clueless.'

20

JJ, after some persuasion and a couple of phone calls, ushered Harry out of the office and took him across the road for something to eat. Harry wanted to know everything, and the more he heard, the more depressed he got. He picked morosely at a salad, while JJ wolfed down a full Ulster fry. Afterwards they adjourned to their old haunt, the Crown, and sat up at the bar, JJ on Guinness and Harry on orange juice. JJ clocked Harry looking around at the lunch-time drinkers with a face on him like a Presbyterian.

'Den of iniquity, eh, Harry?' JJ said, raising his glass.

'No . . . not at all,' Harry replied, not very convincingly.

JJ checked his watch. Then looked to the door. He winked at Harry. 'It'll be fine.'

Harry nodded uncertainly, then sipped his orange. 'Here's Lily now.'

Harry turned to see a diminutive, middle-aged woman with dirty blond hair hurrying across the bar towards them. She had, apparently, done his television make-up for the best part of twenty years, yet he didn't know her from Adam. Or Eve. She carried a parcel under one arm. She ignored JJ and smiled widely at Harry.

'Harry – how are you?' She gave him a hug.

He hugged her awkwardly back. 'Fine,' he said.

She stood back and looked at him. 'You don't remember me at all, do you, Harry?' Harry shook his head. 'Oh, Harry. We were the best of friends.'

Harry, in the light of that morning's revelations, looked suddenly embarrassed. 'We . . .?'

'*No*, Harry, I'm one of the tiny minority you didn't. Though it wasn't for lack of trying.' She held up the parcel, then set it on Harry's lap. 'I brought this for you.'

Harry looked at it for several moments, then gave a little nervous chuckle and opened it up. He delved inside, then smiled at them both as he produced the first of several video tapes.

'Tonight, Harry McKee,' JJ said with a flourish, 'this is your life.'

When Ruth finally arrived home, late that afternoon, laden down with parcels, Harry had already watched the video tapes several times. As bad as they were, he couldn't drag himself away from them. He was like a moth to a naked flame. He sweated, he cringed, he hid behind a cushion. He stood upstairs for a while to escape the full horror of it, but it dragged him down again.

Ruth was putting her bags down in the kitchen when she heard the theme from *What's Cookin'?*, and she knew immediately that the game was up. '*Fuck,*' was her considered reaction.

She walked with some trepidation into the lounge. Harry was hunched forward in an armchair, his eyes on the screen, but most of his face hidden by his cupped hands. He was shaking his head in disbelief. Ruth looked at the screen. Harry was in a green suit, with a green tie. She remembered this one. He was standing in a supermarket, with a crowd of shoppers behind him.

'*. . . Part two of our Saint Patrick's Day special live from . . . Downpatrick.*' He smiled cheesily to camera. '*As you know, all afternoon we've been meeting members* *of the public who happen to be called Patrick.'* He turned to the audience. *'Now, sir, you score double points, because your name is . . .'*

'Patrick Fitzpatrick.'

'And your father's name?'

'My father's name was Patrick Fitzpatrick also.'

'And your mother's name was . . .?'

'Patricia.'

'So that's Patrick Fitzpatrick and his wife Patricia Fitzpatrick and his son is also Patrick Fitzpatrick. Marvellous. You have a son yourself, don't you, Patrick?'

'Yes, I do. His . . .'

Harry moved along to put the microphone before a sullenfaced teenager. *'And what's your name?'*

'Jeremy.'

'Excellent,' said Harry.

Ruth came and stood by her husband. She put a hand on his shoulder. He looked round. 'I'm so embarrassed,' he said. 'Why didn't you . . .?'

'Oh, Harry, I don't know. The doctor thought it best not to expose you to . . .'

'The full horror of it.' He looked back to the screen.

'Now, madam,' he was saying, *'what does the saint mean to you?'*

'I think he's very sexy,' said a woman with a face like a congealed sore.

'Sexy?' Harry said, surprised.

'*Yeah, that Roger Moore's lovely.*'

'*Not* The Saint, *Saint Patrick . . .*'

Harry sat back in his chair and shook his head.

'I'm sorry,' Ruth said.

'I thought people were looking at me because I was respected as a . . .' It petered out. He looked up at her, sitting on the arm of his chair now, her hand still on his shoulder. 'They want me to go and see them.'

'You spoke to them?'

Harry nodded. 'Indirectly. They want me to go back, to start again.' He nodded at the screen. 'I can't do *that*, how could I ever do *that*?'

She squeezed his shoulder. 'Harry, it's television. It's entertainment, it's funny, informative, if it makes one person laugh – and sometimes it does – well, doesn't that make it all worthwhile?'

He wasn't convinced.

'What do you *want* to do?' she asked.

'Hide.'

They talked about it for quite a while. All through dinner, and on into the evening. Billy sulked in his bedroom. Eventually she took some supper up to him on a plate. 'What's all the big pow-wow about?' he asked, barely looking up from his PlayStation.

'They've asked your father to go back to work.'

205

'Why, are they short on the vegetable counter?'

'Don't, Billy. It's a good thing.'

'Oh, sure.'

'Well, it gets him out of your hair.'

'Yeah. Back to the old wanker.'

'You mean you like the newer version?'

'I didn't say that. Besides, you're the one is getting soft.'

'Me?'

'*You.*'

'I *am not*. Sure isn't the whole point of this thing to get him back to normal, then when it gets to court the magistrate won't have any excuse *not* to chuck him out. Isn't that what you want?'

'It certainly is.'

'Right, then eat your supper and stop your complaining. Everything is going according to plan.'

21

Three days later Ruth gave Harry a lift to the television station. She'd even taken him out and bought him a new suit – not too expensive, mind – because he'd lost so much weight he no longer fitted his old ones. She looked upon it as an investment in the future. *Her* future.

He was nervous and jittery all the way over. It reminded her of when she'd given him a lift to that first interview with Frankie Woods, all those years ago. She wondered how her life would have been if she'd not encouraged him to go for it, told him to stick with his job in the paper. Would they have stayed happy?

Here I am doing exactly the same again.

But it's for your benefit. Get him fit – get him out.

Think positive.

She tried to, but, God love him, he looked so uncomfortable. She parked a little way down the street from the station, having had long experience of Ronnie the security guard and his exhaustive scrutiny of every car that sought entrance to the company car park.

As Harry got out, she hopped round to his side, straightened his tie, then gave him a peck on the cheek.

'You look good,' she said.

'You should see me insides.'

'I'd rather not. You'll be fine. Knock 'em dead.'

He smiled at her, but didn't move. He gazed at her, his eyes searching for something. It made her feel uncomfortable. 'What?' she said.

'Nothing.' He shook his head. One thing at a time. 'Right, here goes.'

He turned and walked the few dozen yards back up the street to the station. She was going to give him a final, encouraging wave, but he didn't look back. She shrugged and climbed back into the car. She bit at her nails. She'd been doing a lot of that recently. As she turned the engine on, Cliff Richard came booming out and she snapped a 'Shut up!' And then apologized to him.

There was a small Portakabin to the side of the security gate into which all visitors were directed.

Harry pushed the door open. There was a solitary desk inside, and a small bank of television monitors giving differing views of the car park and the reception area beyond. A thick-set man with a gold-braid-encrusted military uniform sat behind the desk reading a copy of *Guns and Ammo* and sipping a coffee. He looked up as Harry came in, then sniffed delicately at the steam coming off his mug. 'Ah,' he said, 'I love the smell of coffee in the morning . . . it smells of chicory.'

Harry looked a little more bewildered than usual. 'I . . .'

'Who're you here to see, Mr . . .?'

'McKee. Harry McKee. I'm here to see Frank Woods.'

Ronnie spun the visitors book around and then jabbed a chubby nail-to-the-quick finger at the different columns. 'Name, rank and serial number.'

Harry lifted a pen and filled the sheet in perfectly. Ronnie spun the book back round and examined it approvingly. 'Very good, Mr Magee. Just straight through to reception.'

'Thank you.'

'Thank *you*.'

Harry didn't need to go as far as reception. The moment he stepped out of the Portakabin a burly man with frizzy hair enveloped him in a bear hug. Harry gasped, his arms flailing as he struggled for air.

'Harry! Welcome back!'

His accent was American, his chins multiple, his eyes wide.

As he untangled himself from the embrace Harry saw a line of girls, and one young man, waiting to greet him as well.

'Th-thank you,' Harry managed.

'C'mon then, Harry – meet the team!' Frankie Woods – he *presumed* it was Frankie Woods – beckoned him forward. Harry moved reluctantly to the top of the line. 'They're the best in the business, Harry, they keep us on the air five days a week, fifty weeks a year. This is Linda . . .' Harry began shaking hands. 'Janice . . .'

'Hi,' said Harry.

'Mark, Gail, Roisin, Faye . . .'

'I'm sorry . . . I don't remember any of you.'

'You should do,' Frankie boomed, 'you've slept with them all.'

Harry's jaw dropped. They all looked away, embarrassed, except for Mark who stepped forward with an urgent, 'We were both drunk, nothing happened.'

Before he could respond, Frankie clamped an arm around Harry and began to walk him towards the studio. His 'crew' fell into line behind them. 'Harry,' Frankie said, 'Harry, it's so good to see you.' He was all charm, but there was a hint of desperation about him. 'People love you, Harry. We can't move in our office for bags of letters asking when you're coming back. This new guy, they're switching off in droves.'

They walked up the steps into reception. A pretty young receptionist smiled across. Harry smiled nervously back.

'Harry, people have spent so many years with you, you're part of their *lives*.' Frankie was giving it everything. He'd already sweated through his shirt. He was stroking Harry's arm now. The rest of the team trailed obediently behind.

'I know this wasn't what you dreamt about when you were younger,' Frankie continued, 'you were full of fire and determined to change the world – but, Harry, people don't like change. They like to switch on in the morning and know that their Harry is going to be smiling out at them.'

They were heading down a corridor now. Each side of it was hung with photographs of Harry with different celebrities. Harry could only place a handful of them.

'Sure, you might miss the odd word on the autocue; sure, you might drop the odd egg now and again, but that's part of what they love, we know that now.'

The whole group came to a halt outside a set of security doors. It said STUDIO – LIVE above them. Frankie gave Harry one final squeeze. 'It's what the people want, Harry,' he said, then opened the doors with a flourish.

The studio.

Cameras. Lights. Action. He was instantly soaked in sweat.

Immediately everyone stopped what they were doing and, with just a little encouragement from the floor manager, proceeded to give Harry a slightly spontaneous round of applause.

A sea of faces.

A wave of emotion.

And a sudden surge of panic.

'Welcome home, Harry!'

'All right, big lad!'

'Yow! The Big Mac's back!'

They crowded around him. Strangers, smiling, patting, shaking, welcoming, questioning; even Michael Bay, his replacement, came across in his white pinny and begrudgingly shook hands.

The lights were bright, everyone was talking at once.

His throat was dry. He began to feel dizzy. He just needed space. Didn't they know? Didn't they understand?

His head began to spin. He staggered. He was

smiling and trying to stop himself from throwing up at the same time. He couldn't breathe. His shirt was too tight. His heart was racing. He was in the eye of the storm.

It was too much. *Too* much.

'I can't do this,' Harry said.

'What?' Frankie asked.

'I CAN'T DO THIS!'

Harry turned on his heel, pushed through his admirers and hurried back out into the corridor.

They all stood looking expectantly at the swing doors for several moments, some of them laughing, thinking it was good old Harry up to his tricks again, that he would burst through with a big laugh, but they remained resolutely closed.

Frankie, the panic now rising in him as well, banged through the doors and bowled along the corridor in Harry's wake. He didn't dare look at the photographs on the wall. He knew that Harry after Harry after Harry would be laughing down at him. He hurried on. He wanted to let Harry go, but he'd no choice. *No choice*. This was his future. His life. What was he going to do if he couldn't lure Harry back, return to the States? It had been thirty years. He knew no one. And would probably be arrested the moment he stepped off the plane. It had been thirty years, but they'd still be after him. He couldn't go back. He was settled here. He had three failed marriages behind him, a speedboat, and two children. He needed Harry.

Frankie raced through reception, then burst out into the car park.

Harry was standing just beyond the shadow of the building, tie loosened, taking in great gasps of air.

As Frankie approached, Harry turned and pursed his lips apologetically. 'I'm sorry,' he said, 'it was just too much . . .'

'I know, I know,' Frankie said, raising calming hands. 'It's a lot to take in. It's just a matter of getting used to it. Any new job is like that.'

'No, it's more than that . . .'

Frankie was having trouble keeping a lid on his panic. 'Harry, please . . . we're depending on you.' He grasped Harry's hand and pumped it. 'What is it? What do you want?'

'I don't *want* anything.'

'I know I've been bad to you in the past, but I can change . . . just come back to us.'

Harry pulled his hand away. 'You don't under-stand! I can't *remember* how to do it.'

'It doesn't matter! A monkey . . . I mean, if it's the money . . .'

'It's not the money. It's the cameras, the lights, the people, I can't remember any of it!'

'It doesn't matter! We can make it work for us!' He was up close now. Harry, worried about another bear hug, took a step back. 'I've it all planned, Harry . . .' Frankie continued, a bundle of excited energy. 'We hear "Thanks for the Memories", we see lotsa old clips, then – "Do you remember these – 'cause Harry doesn't!" We could . . . we could get you an Afghan . . . coat, dog, whatever, get you a perm, we could do a quiz, bring on previous guests, see if you can guess what they do, it'll be sensational!'

'No! I'm not some sort of freak!'

'Yes, you are! I mean – people will be fascinated. We've got to exploit . . . *explore* that.'

'You don't understand . . .'

This time Frankie lost it. He grabbed Harry by the lapels and twisted them in his pudgy fingers. 'I do understand!' he bellowed. 'For fuck's sake, Harry, what are you going to do with the rest of your life, sit at home and vegetate? This is the chance of a lifetime, Harry. Don't turn your back on it, don't turn your back on us! We need you, Harry!'

Their eyes locked.

Then slowly, slowly, Frankie lightened his grip on the lapels, and carefully smoothed them down. 'C'mon, Harry,' he said softly. 'What harm can it do? Give it a go. If you really don't like it, walk away, but at least try.'

Harry looked about the car park. There was nothing moving. A sparrow ran along the ground. There was a plane in the sky. He took a deep breath. What *was* he going to do? He couldn't remember anything before he was eighteen, but it didn't mean that he *was* eighteen. He was saggy and middle-aged and confused and numb and constantly embarrassed, like the world was in on a big secret, like it was sniggering at him from behind a cupped hand.

What if his memory *never* came back?

Was he doomed to go through the rest of his life constantly on the back foot? Weighed down by fear and indecisiveness? Fearing what was round every corner? Scared of looking stupid and frightened of modern household appliances?

And alone?

He was at the bottom of a deep, dark well and no one was offering to pull him out. Not Ruth. Certainly not Billy. He was being divorced. For all he knew he could be out on the street in a few days. The only person offering him anything was standing right in front of him.

No, dammit.

Why should I? Why lie down and roll over?

WHY?

He had to start somewhere. Dig foundations. Not hide from the Daleks.

Go for it. Go for life. Make something happen.

That was it! Rebuild! Become Meccano.

He turned his attention back to Frankie. The big curly haired producer was almost quaking with anticipation, with fear. Harry took a deep breath. 'Okay,' he said, 'I'll give it a go.'

'*Brilliant*, Harry!' Frankie clamped a hand down on Harry's shoulder.

'But we do it straight. We do it straight or we don't do it at all.'

Frankie nodded calmly, although inside there were fireworks going off. 'Okay. Have it your way.'

Harry smiled, at last. It was all the encouragement Frankie needed. He flung his arms around him and gave him the mother of all bear hugs. 'Oh, Harry!' he exclaimed. 'This is going to be *great*!'

'Okay,' said Harry, as he finally managed to free himself.

'Would you wear flares?' Frankie asked suddenly.

'No,' said Harry.

22

Claire had a part-time job in Club Mix, a small, specialist record store on Great Victoria Street. The idea was that it would help pay the bills, but she bought so many CDs on discount from it that she usually ended up going cap in hand to her dad at the end of every month when the rent fell due. Lately she'd been going to her mum, and getting a harder time of it.

She was a good-looking girl. She had become used to ignoring the occasional spotty teenager or mildewed pervert staring through the shop window at her. So it was a few minutes before she realized it was her father who'd been standing there for so long, watching her every move.

She waved him in and he entered, somewhat furtively. She turned the music down.

'Hiya, Daddy!'

'*Hi Karate!*' Harry responded with a wink, but the old advert was lost on her. To hide his sudden embarrassment he began to flick through the boxes of CDs displayed below the counter. The names and titles were, without exception, meaningless.

'What're you doing in this neck of the woods?' Claire asked.

'Oh . . . just passing. I was wondering, do you have anything that involves a tune and lyrics? Maybe a nice love song? What about something by Leo?'

'Has Leo DiCaprio made a record?'

'Leo *Sayer*.'

She looked at him blankly. 'Sorry, Daddy, lost me there.'

He flicked on through the discs. 'Your mother used to love records.' His eyes flitted up, then down again. 'She used to love me.' There was no response from Claire. 'At this point, you're supposed to say she still does.'

'Oh, Daddy . . .'

The shop door opened and an earnest-looking kid in a black trench coat entered. Claire hurried back behind the counter. Moments later three schoolgirls came in, giggling, and began to enquire about new releases. Harry said he should go on.

'You're not going anywhere,' Claire scolded. 'Lunch. Fifteen minutes. See you outside.'

'No, it's okay, I'll . . .'

'Be there.'

He was there. She brought along sandwiches from Julie's Kitchen. They sat on the steps of the City Hall and munched away.

'In my day,' Harry said, holding up his big thick wholemeal chicken salad sandwich, 'we would have called these doorstops.'

'We still do,' Claire laughed, spraying him with crumbs.

He told her about Frankie Woods and the job offer. She thought he'd done the right thing. That it would do him the world of good.

'But all I do is bake buns and talk nonsense.'

'So does Mum, and she doesn't get paid a fortune for it. What does she think?'

'I haven't told her yet.'

She nodded. He was confused. On the one hand Ruth was being perfectly nice to him, and on the other she was divorcing him. Sometimes he caught her watching him, and she'd suddenly look embarrassed, or giggle or look thoughtful, but she never looked like she hated him, like she wanted him out of the house, even though it was obvious she . . .

'Dad,' Claire said, 'sometimes it's a mistake to think too much.'

'I'm not . . .'

'I can tell. You've got that faraway look you always warned *me* about. Do you not remember . . . no, of course you don't.' She laughed. He laughed. 'When I was a kid, when I was going through my *why are we here* and *how can I save the planet* phase, that's what you used to say to me: *Don't think too much, kid, have a crisp.*'

'Did it work?'

'It used to annoy the crap out of me. But I kind of appreciate it now. What I think you meant was, you can waste half your life worrying about things you're never going to get an answer to or have the power to affect. So worry about the little things, and the big things will take care of themselves.'

'God, this sounds like *The Waltons*.'

'The what?'

He started to explain, but she burst into laughter. Of course she remembered *The Waltons*. They were still being repeated on cable.

She was such a nice, friendly girl. She chatted about her job, her studies, her exams, her hopes. He didn't say much. He stared at her. She was beautiful and perfect. How was that? When he was obviously such a calamity?

You're the only one in the country who doesn't know what a shit you've been.

You've been on every front page, you've been arrested, you're getting divorced, you're a laughing stock.

It's all there in black and white, you drunken slob.

He tried to recommission the sudden burst of confidence that had led him to once again embrace his television career not more than a couple of hours before, but it was gone, its presence as fleeting as a gazelle on a battlefield.

He shivered. He felt so . . . small.

Claire saw, and put a hand on his knee. 'Everything's going to be okay, Daddy,' she said.

'Can I have that in writing?'

'Dad – what do you expect? You've slept with everything that moves.' She sighed. 'You loved each other once.' She hugged him. He smiled sadly. She let him go. He shrugged. 'Oh, Dad – you really don't know what's going on, do you?'

'I'm getting divorced, that's what I know.'

'It's more than that – or it *was* like that. Look – this is what I think. Mum, and Billy – they don't really trust you because you've been such a shit in the past.'

'Was I that bad . . .?'

'Yes, you were.'

'How come you . . .?'

'Because I moved out. You were fine in small doses, okay?'

'Okay.'

'Now Mum's got you kind of back to where you were before, and I think she really, really, deep, deep down wants to give you a second chance, but she just can't quite bring herself to.' He nodded forlornly. 'Dad – it's not enough to just sit there looking gormless. If you want to keep her you have to get out there and win her, win her back. Do you get it, Dad? You have to go back to the start and make her fall in love with you.'

Harry blinked thoughtfully into the afternoon air. Then turned puzzled eyes on his daughter. 'Gormless?' he said.

23

Harry wanted to do something subtle, but Claire was adamant. 'You haven't the time, Dad. You've just over a week to prove you aren't the shit everyone thinks you are.'

'I don't *care* what everyone else thinks. I care what *she* thinks.'

'Well, a bunch of flowers and saying "excuse me" after you burp isn't going to do it for her. You need something big and bold. You need to make a statement, like the Declaration of Independence was a statement.'

'I really don't think that's the most suitable allusion, Claire.'

'You know what I mean. It's not the kid gloves, Dad, it's the bloody pickaxe.'

Claire's final exam had come and gone – mostly gone, according to her – and she was now mad keen to help. It was a little after 9 AM on Day One of the campaign to win back Ruth's heart. They were the only customers in the Texas Homecare superstore in Bangor. He'd never been in a shop this big. Do-it-yourself goods were stacked on shelves half a mile long and almost as high; they seemed to disappear into a slight mist that hid the ceiling and hung over the whole vast warehouse like a warning to get busy. He felt like he was in an episode of *Land of the Giants*.

'Do you think we should ask Billy to help?' Harry asked, following Claire down one of half a dozen aisles featuring paints of every conceivable shade.

'Daddy, for God's sake, open your eyes.'

'I just . . .'

'Let me worry about him. You concentrate on Mum. If she falls, he'll follow. Like a pack of dominoes.'

He thought about correcting her, but she was already gone, whizzing her trolley down the next aisle.

Ruth and Billy had left first thing to go up to Belfast and wouldn't return until late afternoon. A drumming lesson.

When Harry had said, 'Just one?' Billy had thrown one of his drumsticks at him.

'Be careful,' Ruth had scolded, 'you'll put his eye out,'

'That was the intention.'

He'd watched them go, then phoned Claire. There was a lot of work to do. They were aware that their plan was ambitious. 'Who dares wins,' was Claire's take on it.

When they finally arrived home they stacked the paint outside the front door, then went in search of paint brushes and ladders, which they unearthed eventually under piles of boxes in the garage. Harry fetched his collection of David Bowie albums from the roof space. Then they set to work.

Pretty soon Claire decided that Harry's artistic eye was stigmatized, and took his brush off him. She returned to the garage, rummaged about for five minutes, and emerged with a shovel, which she thrust into his hands, and then pointed him towards the top of the garden.

'You have an hour,' she said crisply, 'then you can come back and help me with this.'

Harry said, 'Don't you think this is a bit over the top?'

'Yes,' said Claire, and gave him a gentle push.

They toiled all morning and all afternoon. Harry

wore a pair of greasy overalls some gardener had left behind in the days when they bothered to keep the house and its grounds up to scratch.

They were certainly making a big bold statement.

Two big bold statements.

He wasn't quite sure what that statement was, but Claire assured him that Ruth would be bowled over.

Or *he* would be, then struck about the head with a hammer.

Claire, perched on a ladder, shouted up encouragement from time to time.

He waved back.

It was great getting stuck in like this after so many weeks – and probably years – of inactivity. He loved feeling the sweat roll down his back, he loved the fact that his muscles were aching. He felt like Charles Bronson.

Claire took a break from her painting long enough to approve Harry's handiwork in the garden, then suggested hauling up smooth white pebbles from the seashore to emphasize its outline. Harry huffed and puffed about the legwork involved, though he agreed it made sense. When he had finished they stopped for a cup of tea and a Harvest Crunch bar, then he joined Claire at the painting. She was up the ladder doing the delicate work, he remained at the bottom providing the broad strokes.

They were almost, *almost* finished, when the car pulled into the driveway. It stopped suddenly just inside the gates, as if it was taking a deep breath, then progressed slowly up towards the house. Harry stood at the bottom of the ladder, paint-spattered; Claire stood halfway up, a headscarf tied on to protect her hair, beaming. They gave each other the thumbs-up as Ruth stopped the car.

There was another pause, as they waited for the doors to open. Harry glanced nervously at Claire, but she was smiling like there was absolutely no doubt about Ruth's reaction.

Billy stepped out first. He stood, staring up at the house. 'Ho-ly shit,' he said.

Ruth climbed out. She looked at Harry, at his smile, and then to the nightmare before her.

She said, 'Why have you painted the cover of *Aladdin Sane* on the front of my house?'

She stared at the huge pink-tinged face with its jagged red, black and blue lightning streak and the swept-back, slightly quiffed red hair.

'We . . .'

'Why would I want a twenty-foot picture of David Bowie on the wall of my house?'

'Because it's the first album I ever bought you, and I loved you then as much as I love you now.'

She looked at him, and she wanted there to be

228

anger and rage and embarrassment, she wanted to rail about the stupidity and the rateable value of what would shortly be *her* property, but instead something tiny, something fragile, way down deep inside her, seemed to break and for a moment she found it difficult to get her breath.

She fought against it, whatever *it* was.

Claire came down the ladder and skipped up to her. 'What do you think, Mum?' she asked eagerly. 'Class, isn't it?'

'I think I need a drink.'

'Make mine a double,' said Billy.

'I think it's lush,' Claire said eagerly. 'It just says so much. It's from the heart, Mum.'

'Has anyone alerted air traffic control?' Billy asked.

'But . . . but what will the neighbours say?' Ruth asked in desperation. Really, it was the last thing she was concerned about.

He was up beside her now, looking up at his master work. Or Claire's master work, mainly. 'What does it matter what they think? Do *you* like it?'

'I . . .' There was such a hopeful look in Harry's eyes that she found it difficult to put her horror into words. 'I suppose . . . it's okay,' she said finally.

Harry beamed. Ruth rolled her eyes at Billy. He rolled them back. She started for the front door, but

Harry gently caught her arm. He glanced at Claire for encouragement, and she winked back.

'Ahm, Ruth, I have some news for you.'

Ruth looked at Claire, then back to Harry. She made a mental note to slap Claire around the head for conspiring against her. 'What, Harry?'

'I've decided to go back to work. *What's Cookin'?* and all that malarkey.'

'That's good, Harry. I'm pleased.' She smiled and went to move on, but he still wouldn't let go of her arm. *'What?'*

'I thought maybe, y'know, we could go out . . . celebrate. Or something. Just the two of us. Dinner.'

His big expectant eyes. Claire's twinkling encouragement. Billy's burning into the back of her.

Christ, what was she supposed to do?

She just wanted inside, and she just wanted that drink. A nice big stiff one.

'No, Harry. Not tonight. I've . . .'

'Tomorrow night?' came in like a flash.

She took a deep breath. 'Okay, Harry.'

'Really?'

'Really.'

He smiled shyly. 'I'll press my pants.'

Then he did the oddest thing. He winked at her. A big, broad, stage wink. Then nodded behind him, back up the garden.

'What are you . . .?'

He did it again, winked, then nodded up the garden. Then he let her go, and walked on into the house.

Her brow crinkled as she followed the direction he'd been nodding in, along the lawn and up the slope towards the back fence . . . and there it was.

A heart, cut into the grass, and outlined with white rocks.

It was the stupidest, crassest, most vulgar act of shop-window sentimentalism she'd ever experienced. And unbidden, uninvited, gate-crashing like the worst drunk, a tear sprang from her eye.

'Oh, Harry,' Ruth whispered, 'you silly bugger.'

24

Ruth spent that night fidgeting. Pacing, tapping her fingers, combing her hair, biting her nails, she hardly slept. What was going on? Why was she feeling so strange? She should be elated, she was on the verge of finally defeating him and now she had friggin' butterflies in her stomach.

What was she thinking of?

Why had she let herself be suckered into dinner on the strength of an embarrassing painting and some gardening?

Going out would only make it harder on him when push came to shove.

Serves him right, after all the years of shit. Let him wallow in it.

But just because he was cruel, doesn't mean you have to be.

She was relieved to find Harry was already away out by the time she made it downstairs the next morning. Billy said he'd gone to the TV studio. Then he asked her what the hell she was playing at. She told him to clam up and eat his breakfast.

She didn't want to think about it any more. She threw herself with abandon into the hoovering, the washing, the ironing and even at one stage considered cleaning the toilets, but she drew back at the last moment. Instead she buried herself in a packet of Rich Tea biscuits. Then she had a Cornetto from the freezer. And a packet of Tayto Smoky Bacon crisps. She locked herself in her room and watched TV, but avoided *Oprah, Ricki* and all of the other chat shows.

She didn't need advice.

She knew she'd got herself into this mess.

She really didn't want to go out for dinner with Harry McKee.

Plus, she had nothing to wear.

Ruth managed a nap in the afternoon, and felt better for it.

Just take it easy. Go with the flow. It's your life. Nobody can tell you what to do.

She took a bath, and relaxed in it for an hour. She tied her hair up, and tried on a trouser suit she hadn't worn for a long time. He hadn't said where they were going. She didn't want to overdo it. Or under. She ditched the trouser suit. She put on a mid-length skirt and ankle boots. She let her hair down again.

It was a little before seven when she eventually made it downstairs, with her hair up. Claire was sitting in front of the TV, concentrating harder than any sane person should on *Emmerdale*. Billy was on the sofa beside her.

'You seem to be spending an awful lot of time here,' Ruth said, 'for someone who was so keen to move out.'

'Mummy,' Claire said, 'that's not fair.'

'Mmmmm,' said Ruth. 'Where's your father?'

'He's . . .' Billy began, then Claire elbowed him, and he reluctantly concluded with, 'outside.'

Ruth put her hands on her hips. 'Do you mind telling me what's going on?'

'What do you mean?'

'Furtive is the word, I believe.'

'Mummy, please. You're so paranoid these days.' Then Claire tutted and got up. 'Well,' she said, 'if it makes you happy.' She signalled for Ruth to follow her, led her out of the lounge, through the kitchen and towards the back door. Billy trailed behind, feigning non-interest.

It was, clearly, prearranged. Probably triggered by the flush of the toilet or her footsteps on the stairs.

As she stepped out onto the weed-strewn yard, there was the sudden roar of an engine and Harry came flying around the corner behind the wheel of . . .

A soft-top TR7.

It screeched to a halt in a cloud of dust and nettles. And rust.

'Jesus Christ,' said Ruth, 'when is it going to end?'

Claire clapped her hands together, and jumped up and down as Harry leapt out of the car and hurried round to Ruth's side. He opened the passenger door with a flourish. 'Isn't it lush, Ruth!' He grinned. 'I always wanted one of these – and so did you. It's second-hand like, but isn't it brill?'

'It's . . . where did you . . .?'

'Don't worry! I found my bank account! There's over a *hundred pounds* left in it! Get in, come on!'

And she did.

Harry rubbed his hands together, winked at Claire, tried to ruffle Billy's hair, but he ducked away, then jogged back round to the driver's side.

Ruth shook her head at her daughter. 'I feel ridiculous,' she said.

'You *look* beautiful,' Claire said. 'Have a good . . .'

There wasn't time to finish. Harry took off at speed, missing the driveway completely and careering across the overgrown lawn towards the gates, then through them, and onto the road, his foot barely touching the brakes.

As the little sports car disappeared into the distance, Billy came up beside Claire. 'I hope you know what you're doing,' he said flatly.

'Kind of,' said Claire.

They drove the four miles to Bangor with the wind in their hair, then parked and walked along the front. He remembered a broad promenade overlooking a delightful bay, but it had been narrowed to make way for a car park, and the bay itself was now mostly invisible, hidden by a vast marina. Hundreds of yachts clinked in the sea breeze. It was a beautiful, fresh, warm evening. He looked back along Queen's Parade, opposite the promenade, hoping to spot the old fleapit of the Queen's Cinema, where they'd spent many a night in the back row, or the Dolphin Hotel, or the Queen's Court nightclub, or the amusement arcades, but they were all gone, all demolished. They walked further towards the old outdoor Pickie Pool where he'd half frozen to death along with thousands of other kids in the summer, but it too was gone.

There was a kids' playground now. There was a boating lake which you could paddle around in huge white swans.

'It's all gone,' Harry said.

'It's all new, Harry. Things change.'

They both thought, *people change*, but neither of them said it.

'What about the Tonic?'

'It's gone too. Flats for old people.'

'That's where I first kissed you.'

'That's where you first *pawed* me.'

'You didn't object.'

'I was bored. It was *Where Eagles Dare*, as I recall. And you certainly did.'

'I thought I was Clint Eastwood. And you thought you were . . .'

'Ingrid Pitt.'

'Jesus, you've a good memory.'

'It's as well one of us has.' She shook her head. She glanced about her. She was suddenly uncomfortable. This was going well. Too well. She needed to be detached. 'I thought you were taking me to dinner.'

'I am.'

He took her hand, before she could object, and led her back along to Queen's Parade. A couple of minutes later they were queueing in a chip shop.

'This isn't quite what I had in mind,' Ruth said.

Harry was examining the menu for something even vaguely healthy, but everything bar the cans of Coke and the chips was covered in batter.

'Harry, we don't have to eat here . . .'

'We do . . . we always used to . . .'

The heels of her boots were sticking to the floor. She was glad she hadn't worn the ball gown. She couldn't remember the last time they'd eaten chips on the hoof. It was quite exciting, in its own way.

They got a fish supper between them, then drove along the coast to Helen's Bay and sat eating it as they looked out over a sea they could see. At least, *she* sat eating it; Harry picked at the fish, and then only the white bits, and ignored the chips completely. When they'd finished he wrapped the greasy paper up and went to find a bin.

They sat on, chatting with relative ease.

It grew dark, rain clouds gathered, but it was pleasantly warm and they preferred to sit with the top still down.

'If you had your life to live over again,' Harry asked out of the blue, 'would you change it?'

Ruth shrugged. 'Bits of it, I suppose. Or maybe not. Sometimes you have to make a difficult journey to get to where you want to be.'

Harry laughed. 'Which famous philosopher said that?'

'*Jung*,' said Ruth. 'At least, Debbie Young – used to take us in the Guides.'

They both smiled at the weakness of it.

They looked at each other, then Harry reached across and kissed her on the lips. It was just the lightest brush, and then he pulled back.

She didn't know what . . .

I don't know . . .

Jesus . . .

His lips came again, and this time they lingered, and suddenly Ruth was kissing him back.

Above them it thundered, and rain began to pour.

Harry's hand snaked out, searching for the button to activate the roof. He found it, pressed it, but nothing happened. He pressed it again, but still nothing. On the third attempt Ruth pulled away. He cupped her face in his hands and tried to kiss her again, but she resisted.

Christ, what am I doing!

How could I . . .

What on earth . . .

'It's raining,' she said weakly.

'Forget the rain.'

He tried to kiss her again, but there was such an

urgency about it that it was suddenly easier for her to resist. 'I *can't* forget it.'

She turned away. She was getting soaked.

What have I done!

It wasn't just the rain, there were suddenly tears cascading down her face. She had *kissed* him. The creature from the black lagoon, the man she abhorred, the man she was getting rid of, and she had enjoyed it, *loved* it.

Oh, the shame.

Oh, the hypocrisy.

Oh, the relief.

Oh, the fucking madness.

Her hand fumbled for the door handle, she pulled it, climbed out.

'Ruth, please!'

The car park was lit by a single lamp post twenty yards away. If she could just get to it she would surely be safe. Like in a kid's game. She hurried towards it, tens of thousands of floodlit raindrops guiding her way. She heard the car door close and footsteps behind her. He caught her, he came through the force field and twirled her round and held her close. He tried to kiss her again, but she turned her face away. He kissed her damp hair, her ear, her cheek, then found her lips again, and they kissed until she forced herself free.

'Don't, Harry . . . *don't*!' she cried. 'God, I can't do this any more!'

'Ruth, just listen . . .'

'I can't! We're not eighteen any more, Harry! We're getting . . .'

'Divorced! I know!'

She wiped at her face. She was suddenly sober, although she hadn't touched a drop. He had intoxicated her. Now it was full-belt hangover.

'You *know*?' she hissed. 'You mean you've been acting all along?'

He held her by the shoulders. She tried to shrug him off, but he held her firm. 'No,' he said, 'of course I don't remember. But it doesn't mean I'm stupid. I *found out*. Ruth, I know what I was! I know what I became! I hate what I've done to you . . . but I'm trying to change!'

She tried to pull away, but couldn't. Her eyes blazed up at him. 'No, Harry! It's too late! I'm sorry, I didn't mean to lead you on . . . but it's *over. Please*, Harry.'

His hands fell suddenly from her shoulders and they stood face to face in the rain.

She didn't owe him anything, least of all an explanation. But he looked so lost, bewildered. 'Harry – maybe if it had been me, my head would have been turned, but it wasn't, it was you, *you*

241

betrayed *us*, not me. And then it happened again and again until I just stopped caring. I stayed for the kids, Harry, but even that's . . .' She shook her head. 'You only live once, Harry.'

'No . . . Ruth . . . no, you only live *twice*.'

'Don't be funny on me now, please.'

'I'm not! We've been given a second chance! We can do this!'

'No, Harry! I've heard it a thousand times! I can't give in again, it'll kill me!'

'And it'll kill me if you don't!' He pulled her to him again. 'I love you, Ruth! Please don't leave me!'

He was crying. She was crying. They hugged in desperation, and somewhere, somehow, his lips found hers again, and this time they were kissing with the passion of so many lost years and nothing could drag them apart.

25

Her head was spinning like that girl's in *The Exorcist*.

What have I done, what am I doing, what have I done, what am I doing, what have I done, what am I doing?

They drove home through the rain, getting soaked even further.

Harry was scarcely any calmer. *I've won her back. Don't push it. I've won her back, don't push it. Relax, relax, relax, relax.*

He had a raging erection. He was a virgin, at least mentally. She was beautiful and lovely and he wanted to enter the Time Tunnel to get home faster. He wanted to scoop her up in his arms and take her to bed.

He was giddy.

She was giddy.

He wasn't speeding, but he went through red lights, he missed turnings, he was halfway home before he realized his lights weren't on and it was suddenly clear why people had been flashing at him for miles. He thought it was some kind of universal acknowledgement that love had found a way, had triumphed against all odds.

She was thinking: *it's only a kiss, it's only a kiss, it doesn't mean anything, it's the heat of the moment, who can blame a girl who hasn't been kissed in years from succumbing to a moment of passion?*

It was wonderful.

It was dreadful.

She was ashamed.

She was elated.

They came through the front door and he took hold of her again and they kissed in the hall, dripping everywhere.

She was absolutely lost in it when Billy said suddenly: 'What're you gonna do now? Take him upstairs and screw him?'

And with that they came apart, the spell broken. Billy tramped past them, then took the stairs one at a time, a third of his usual pace. Ruth tried to say something after him, but what was there to say? Suddenly she felt small and guilty.

Harry took her hand. 'Let me have a word with him,' he said. She nodded vaguely. She was frightened now. Everything had been so certain. She was going to live again and had been desperately looking forward to it, and now she'd put all of that at risk over something as stupid as a bit of fumbling in a car park.

Like kids.

Like Harry.

Shit!

And yet she wanted to kiss him again. She watched him hurry up the stairs after Billy, then dashed into the kitchen and poured herself a drink. Then she tipped it down the sink.

No alcohol. No hiding. Deal with it. Face it. Face it!

Billy was already in behind his drum kit and bashing away when Harry entered his room. He stood before him. 'Billy, I know this hasn't been easy . . .'

Still thumping, Billy shouted: 'I can't hear you!' and looked away.

'Then stop that friggin' racket!' Harry shouted. He leaned forward and ripped the sticks from Billy's surprised hands.

They glared at each other, then Harry remembered he was father, not brother. 'Look,' he said, 'I know this hasn't been easy on you.'

'What is this, *The Waltons?*'

'Billy, I . . .'

'I know what you're going to say,' Billy snapped, 'so give me a break. I'm very happy for you two. I'm glad it's all worked out well in the end, et cetera, et cetera.'

'Billy, nothing's worked out.' Harry sighed. 'Son, I *don't remember*. What it was like. What we were like.'

'You don't remember beating me with a big stick? With a nail in the end?'

'I . . . did that?' said Harry, suddenly appalled.

'No. But you needn't think a paint job and smarm attack is going to make up for a decade of being a shitehawk. Ten years of being a laughing stock because you're on the front page of every Sunday newspaper. Have you any idea how often people ask me what's cookin'? How often people say is your dad that wanker on the TV? Well, here's a clue – twenty times every day, okay? Okay? All right?'

Harry looked at him for several moments, then handed the sticks back – except he didn't let go as Billy grasped them. He held on, then said softly: 'Billy, were you never disappointed in yourself?'

Billy nodded. 'Sure, I was.'

'Do you ever think how you would cope in my situation?'

'Sure, I do. I'd avoid turning into a self-pitying bastard.'

Harry nodded. 'Are you sure you haven't?' he asked quietly, then let go of the sticks. He walked out of the room. Billy snarled something after him, but he couldn't make it out.

Such anger. Such hatred. Ruth had hidden her dislike of him so well, yet now he had real hope that she would get over that. Billy, on the other hand, had never made any effort to hide the fact that he despised his father. *My own son*. He just wanted to pick him up and hug him and tell him what a miracle he was and how much he loved him and how they could be great mates and go to the pictures and play football in the garden and set up a band together. But he knew if he tried to hug him, Billy would call the police.

Harry walked slowly down the stairs, then into the lounge and kitchen, looking for Ruth. He knocked on her bedroom door, but there was no response.

'In here, Harry.'

He moved to his own doorway, and saw that she was sitting on his fold-down bed. The blankets were turned back. She was playing nervously with her hair. She was beautiful and his friend now, but he felt numb; he couldn't get Billy out of his head, the depth of his hatred. He had won half the battle, but would the act of celebration doom him to eventual defeat?

He looked at her, and she looked back, puzzled. Billy.

He had to show that he had changed. That he could stop, and consider, look at the bigger picture.

He wanted to love her, but to love her properly. Without pressure, without confusion.

He felt as if they were on the *Titanic*, and it was sinking, but then by some miracle they were able to patch her up, and survive. It was time to acknowledge the fact that they were alive, not to suddenly strike out for America.

'Is he . . .?' Ruth asked.

'I had a word,' Harry said. 'It's all sorted.'

She nodded. She looked away.

'Well,' Harry said, 'maybe we can go out again.'

Ruth nodded. 'That would be nice.'

'Okay. I'll see you tomorrow.'

Ruth stood quickly. She couldn't believe it. She was getting the brush-off. He had led her up the garden path. She had jumped off the fucking cliff for him and now the complete bastard was . . .

Yet he didn't *look* as if he was giving her the brush-off. There was no evil glint. No gloating. No triumphant smirk. There was, rather, a tremendous sadness about him. She had an inkling that the instant she left the room he would start that odd rocking again.

'Are you all right, Harry?' she asked softly.

He nodded. 'Tired.'

'Okay . . . I'll see you in the morning.' She kissed the top of his head, then hurried from the room.

She went into the kitchen, and this time she did take a drink. She sat at the table drumming her fingers.

She tried to think of the last time she had made love to anyone but herself. She couldn't. It was certainly several years, back in the days when their love-hate thing would explode into torrid, wonderful sex that made her hate him even more when daylight came.

She poured herself another drink and took a notebook and pen from the kitchen drawer.

She wrote: *libido* and *lust*.

Then studied them for anagrams, but without success.

She had let those little words override her common sense. It had been a lucky escape.

Yet what was life about, if it wasn't about making love?

After fifteen minutes and another glass of Smirnoff, she went up to Harry's room. The door was still slightly open and she peered in. He was indeed rocking on the edge of his bed. His eyes were closed and there were tears streaming down his cheeks.

She had thought that he might look up, catch her eye, and invite her in. Or that she might suddenly disrobe, declare that she might as well be shot for a sheep as a lamb, and jump into bed with him. But now there was a lump in her throat, and she knew that to do *anything* other than to tiptoe off to bed would be a terrible, devastating intrusion. She padded gently along to her room.

26

Harry spent the next few days in the studio familiarizing himself with the whole process of live television. Frankie supervised the broadcast of *What's Cookin'?* in the mornings, then lent himself to the re-education of Harry McKee in the afternoons.

Michael Bay, the guest presenter, was aware that he was about to get the heave-ho and was relatively relaxed about it. The restaurant he owned had actually experienced a drop in business since he'd begun to appear on television, the plainest evidence possible of his own inadequacy when it came to performing for the cameras. He longed to get back to the anonymity of his kitchens and if bringing Harry up to scratch on the culinary front would help speed that up, then he was the man to do it.

Harry proved to be a brilliant student. Michael only had to show him something once, and he knew how to do it. And sometimes better. Certainly faster.

'But then you have been doing it for years,' Michael said one afternoon, nodding approvingly at Harry's latest creation. 'Believe me, *that's* instinctive. You may not be able to find it in here . . .' he said, tapping his head, 'but you certainly have it in *here* . . .' and he placed his hand over Harry's heart.

Harry nodded appreciatively, but thought to himself that Michael Bay talked a lot of pish.

Michael took a forkful of Harry's lasagne, chewed, swallowed, then beamed: 'Beautiful, absolutely beautiful. You should make this for your beautiful wife.'

When they'd finished cooking, Frankie came and took him down to wardrobe. He supervised as Harry was fitted with an exuberant red silk shirt, a black leather waistcoat and tight bell-bottomed trousers. Then he was led upstairs to the studio floor where he was put through his paces with half a dozen high-kicking dancing girls. He had to move smoothly through them, smile to camera, wink and say: 'Can I still crack it? Or have I gone off the boil? Find out Monday, 10 AM – don't go away now!' Then groove back through the dancers again.

Harry had agreed to do it once, just to prove it really was as awful as he feared.

Frankie promised that if Harry didn't like it, then they wouldn't use it.

Harry didn't like it. 'I look like a complete friggin' eejit!'

'You're right! You're right, we won't use it.'

And of course he used it. Harry nearly choked on his supper when they broadcast it. Ruth was in hysterics. Billy even managed a smile.

Harry got on the phone and raged down the line at Frankie, about his promise and the fact that he was a slippery lying son of a bitch. He threatened to pull out completely. Frankie apologized. It had been broadcast by mistake. The tapes had been mixed up. That was another lie, but one thing he told Harry was true: the response. There had been dozens and dozens of calls, not only from viewers happy that their Harry was coming back, but from advertisers as well, determined to book space on his comeback.

Frankie was elated. He worked hard to calm Harry down. He increased his money on the spot. He volunteered to give him an executive producer credit which would mean even more money.

'It's not about money,' Harry said.

After Frankie had finished laughing he said: 'Okay,

Harry, it's about being happy, and being respected, and I disrespected you. I'm sorry. It won't happen again.'

They'd shoot some more teasers tomorrow. There'd be no dancing girls. No silk shirts. Just Harry.

Just Harry.

Walter Adair, ex-Assembly Member, ex-husband, ex-next big thing, weaved drunkenly between the cars stuck in Shaftesbury Square's lunch-time grid-lock. He skipped, he slipped, he smiled, he giggled, he cursed, he belched, he proclaimed to the world his genius and his downfall and just when he thought no one was watching he discovered that one person was: Harry McKee, a giant, giant Harry McKee on a giant screen way up above the traffic.

Harry McKee dancing, laughing, pointing *at him*.

Walter Adair screamed in rage and agony.

He ran, and ran, and eventually found a bar that would serve him.

He sat in a dark corner and dreamed of great things, and then plotted terrible things. He rolled home in late afternoon. He sneered at the *For Sale* sign in the garden, then stalked the silent rooms of his home. Tara was now only communicating via her solicitor. His friends, the friends he had partied with, slept with, had not been in touch either. He was a nobody. *Persona non grata*.

He stood in their bedroom, trying to hold back the tears. He entered Tara's walk-in dressing room. She had been in such a rush to leave, and so reluctant to return, that half of her clothes were still there, her dresses, her lingerie. He smelled her everywhere. He held her favourite red outfit to his face. God, he missed her. God, he had been so stupid. Each time he had done the dirty deed he had sworn, never again, you'll get caught.

Yet he kept going back for more.

How could he have been so stupid? He had always known the dangers of discovery, that catastrophe would surely follow.

He pulled the dress away from his face and studied his own reflection in the full-length mirror. He was totally naked.

But he had not been stupid. He had not been *caught*. He had been *exposed*. He had been hung, drawn and quartered on live television without the benefit of a lawyer or a jury.

It was *wrong*.

He hadn't been an angel, but did he deserve this vilification?

NO, HE DID NOT!

He collapsed down to his knees, and then lay on the floor, enveloped in the dress. The drink had made him suddenly tired. He hugged the dress again; he stroked it; she had been a wonderful wife, and would be again. He would win her back. He would . . .

He opened his eyes.

He had fallen asleep. It was dusk outside. The dressing room, shielded from the bedroom window, was in almost complete darkness. He shivered. Something had woken him.

Then he heard it properly: a door slamming. Silence. Then laughter. *Nervous* laughter. A light went on.

Walter gulped with fright, and scrambled to his knees. He shuffled across and carefully pushed the dressing-room door closed. He felt about for his trousers, then cursed as he realized he'd left them outside in the hall. He stood, panting, straining to hear *something*.

Whispers.

Footsteps.

A deep voice said: 'We'll start with the bedrooms.' Then the hall light went on.

Walter began to shake.

Burglars.

Come to strip the house. Come to raid the safe which was hidden away in this very dressing room, like they'd never guess.

Or . . . *Jesus* . . . what if it was *worse* than burglars.

A lynch mob!

Walter shuddered. Belfast was a notably homo-phobic town. He had heard of people like himself being beaten up, even murdered, with no greater justification than their odd sexual orientation.

'No sign of him . . .' echoed around the house.

The intruders were here for *him*!

As far as they were concerned he was a fruit and therefore fair game. Walter would have disputed that he was even bi-sexual. He didn't find men particu-larly attractive. He just liked having orgasms, and he wasn't fussy who with. His divorce lawyer had advised him not to mention this in court, and to move to Thailand.

Walter's heart was beating ninety to the dozen. There were footsteps on the wooden floor of the landing. He was naked in the darkness of his wife's dressing room. If they found him there, like that, they'd beat him to a pulp without question, and then shoot him.

Shoot!

Christ! He had a *gun*.

When there'd been a breakdown in the cease-fire a couple of years back the police had offered him the choice of a full-time bodyguard or his own weapon. He hadn't wanted a cop getting in the way of his lively social life, so he'd gone for the gun. He'd even taken a couple of lessons.

But where will I keep it, in the safe?

No, difficult to get at in a hurry, and the first place they'd look. Somewhere they wouldn't expect, like . . .

In the shoe boxes.

Right here in the dark.

The voices were getting closer.

Walter felt his way along the rack of dresses to where the shoe boxes had once sat right up to shoulder level. They weren't that high now, but there were still some Tara hadn't taken with her. Desperately Walter began to lift them down, one after the other, prising their lids off and slipping his fingers in to feel in and around the shoes. The door to their bedroom opened. The light went on. Jesus, what if his pint pot Imelda had taken the gun with her? He was on the third. The fourth. The fifth . . . cold metal. *The gun!*

Walter ripped it out of the box just as the dressing-room door opened, bathing his naked body in light. Walter raised the pistol in two hands, aimed for the largest of the three silhouettes and screamed: 'Don't move a fucking inch, you motherfuckers! I'll blow your arseholes from here to fucking eternity!'

They froze. There was a moment when he almost blasted them anyway, but he just managed to hold himself in check.

He shifted the gunsight from one to the other.

They were *his*. He had outfoxed them. He was quite within his rights to blast them off the face . . .

'Ah, Mr Adair,' a voice he half recognized said somewhat querulously, 'we were wondering where you were. I, ahm, hope you don't mind, we let ourselves in . . . This is Mr and Mrs Mason . . . the seven o'clock viewing?'

Mr and Mrs Mason nodded hello.

'Of course not,' said Walter, lowering the gun, 'just look around yourselves, anything you need to know I'll be right here.'

He smiled, then pulled the dressing-room door closed.

27

It was the eve of Harry's return to live television. It was also the eve of their divorce becoming absolute. It was an ironic coincidence neither Ruth nor Harry felt able to comment on. They had not kissed since their night out. They had tiptoed nervously around each other, hardly speaking. Not enemies, yet not friends. They were lovers who hadn't made love. They were criminals who hadn't been convicted. They didn't know whether they were coming or going. It was Christmas Eve, in a way, and each was desperate to discover whether Santa would leave presents or coal in the morning, yet they couldn't ask him directly for risk of getting an answer they didn't want.

Ruth had a million things going through her head, and she couldn't tell any of them to Ms Boyle. She sat in her office while she went over the final details, nodding in the appropriate places, but her heart wasn't in it. She didn't know where her heart was, that was the whole bloody problem. Yes, she had had one pleasant evening with Harry, but was that enough to base the rest of her life upon? Of *course* it wasn't.

'Why the long face, Ruth?' Boyle asked.

Ruth made some excuse about being run down, and Boyle gave her some bull about it being the happiest day of her life, and not to think of it as an end, but as a beginning. For the third day in a row Ruth found an excuse not to go home early. She stood in a bookshop for hours. She only left because a middle-aged man tried to hit on her in the self-assertiveness section. She drank coffee, she bought tights. She bought clothes, but told herself she would bring them back, therein convincing herself that she wasn't actually spending any money. She bought six bottles of aftersun, four of them because they were offering extra points on her Boots loyalty card. She was spending *and* saving.

Everything she did, everywhere she went, she couldn't stop thinking about Harry.

About how he was looking grand, and kissing like

a demon. How he was growing in confidence, and kissing like a demon. Even in the few weeks since he came home he had begun to mature into the kind of man she had hoped he would become. And he kissed like a demon.

Tomorrow, we get divorced.

Look at the scales of justice, Ruth – twenty years of torment, against one half-decent night on the town.

There was only one decision.

She arrived home at a little after eight. Claire was standing in the hall waiting for her. 'Keys, please,' she said, holding her hand out. She had her coat on.

'What's going on?' Ruth asked.

'Ask no questions. Hear no lies.' Claire lifted the keys out of her mum's hand, then waved Billy down from where he was sitting halfway up the stairs. 'We're going to the flicks.'

'Under duress,' said Billy glumly.

Claire slapped him playfully on the back of the head, then smiled at Ruth. 'You're wanted – in there,' she said, nodding towards the dining room. Ruth hesitated. 'Go *on*,' said Claire, giving her a gentle push.

Ruth opened the door slowly. It was quite gloomy, and she thought for a moment that one of the bulbs had gone and was wondering where she put the last set she'd bought when she realized it wasn't gloom, but candlelight, and there was Harry standing smiling

at the head of the set table; he was in his dinner
jacket, his tux.

'Harry . . . what's going on . . .?'

He didn't speak. He drew back one of the chairs
and beckoned for her to sit.

'O-kay,' she said. She crossed the room, then Harry
held the chair and moved it in behind her as she
sat. 'What's all this in aid of, Harry?'

'You,' he said.

He turned for the kitchen, then stopped for a
moment to flick a small switch. Immediately a
hundred white Christmas fairy lights blinked on. He
smiled back at her.

When the door closed, Ruth shook her head. She
didn't know whether to be sick or cry. It was an
eighteen-year-old's idea of what a romantic dinner
should be. It was like stumbling into a Mills & Boon
novel. And yet . . . forty million housewives can't
be wrong.

Outside, sitting on a pair of sagging deckchairs,
Claire and Billy watched it all. They had a pair of
binoculars and a bottle of wine.

'This is better than any movie, eh, Billy?' Claire
said as Harry served the dinner.

'Yeah, sure,' Billy responded, his attention focused
more on the roll-up he was preparing. 'How long
does it take laxatives to work?'

'*What*?'

'Relax. I tried. But security was too tight.'

There was a full moon high in the sky. The waves lapped softly against the sea wall across the road behind them. They drank from the bottle and smoked.

'Mum says you went to the TV studio with Dad yesterday,' said Claire.

'I was bored. And even more bored once I was there.'

'Do you think he's trying to get you into show business?'

'No friggin' chance. He tries to force me, I'll run away and join the Foreign Legion.'

'You'd hate the Foreign Legion. You don't like foreign food for a start.'

'The British Legion, then.'

'Okay,' Claire said, the binoculars suddenly clamped back to her eyes like a general in a tank battle. 'That's the first course . . .'

'Jesus, less talking, more eating, they would have been finished ages ago.'

'It's good to talk, Billy.'

'Aye.'

And they were talking. Ruth had relaxed into it with remarkably little effort. It wasn't an endurance test any more. It wasn't like trying to talk to that wide-eyed wee lad she'd brought back from the hospital. They focused on what they knew and shared, rather than what he had forgotten and she never would.

'Wee Johnny Black?' Harry was saying. 'He's a *chiropodist*! Sure wasn't he the one always talking about . . .'

'Sex! That's right! He *was* training to be a gynaecologist. I heard he could do the practical but couldn't handle the theory.'

They laughed together. Harry lifted the bottle of wine and poured Ruth another glass.

She hesitated, then said: 'Aren't you going to have any?'

He shook his head. 'I don't drink, remember?' He poured water for himself, then raised it to her. They clinked glasses. 'You've grown more beautiful,' he said softly. She smiled. He gave a little chuckle.

'What?'

'Nothing.'

'No, what?'

'I was just thinking. I've two children, and I've never been to bed with a woman.'

She blinked.

Don't do it, don't do it, don't do . . .

Oh, fuck it, do it and be done.

She set her glass down, stood up, and came round

to his side of the table. She took his hand. 'Take me to bed then, Harry.'

Outside, Billy wrestled the binoculars off Claire. 'Here we go, here we go, here we go!' he sang.

Claire shushed him. 'I think it's lovely.'

They watched their parents progress out of the dining room and along the hall towards Ruth's bedroom. The light went on. Ruth immediately crossed and closed the curtains. Billy booed. After five minutes the light went off.

'At this point.' Billy said, 'I should phone in a bomb scare.'

'Admit defeat, Billy, they're in love.'

'It ain't over till it's over.' He lifted the wine bottle and gave it a shake. There was only enough left for a couple of slurps each. 'How long do we give them?'

'At their age?' Claire thought for a moment. 'A couple of days.'

They both sniggered, and looked back up to the house. Aladdin Sane stared out at them. Fairy lights blinked on and off. They were sitting in their front garden drinking cheap wine while their parents made love for the first time in years. Anyone would think they were on dope.

Ruth was past the age of lying about sex. 'That was lovely,' she said, and meant it.

Harry shrugged. 'Beginner's luck.'

They lay in the darkness, wrapped in each other. He was a bear of a man, but had been as soft and gentle as a teddy. There had been a lot of passion, a lot of lust, but she was so relieved to find that she was just as happy after the event as before and certainly during. It wasn't like she'd just been frustrated, and now they could go back to war. She felt . . .

Oh, God. In love.

Harry stroked her hair. 'Tomorrow . . .' he began.

'You're on TV, and we get divorced.' His hand stopped the stroking. 'What,' Ruth said softly, 'you think one roll in the hay will change everything?'

Harry tried to swallow, but his throat was suddenly dry. 'Can't it?' he rasped.

She shook her head. 'No, Harry.' Then paused. 'But two might.'

He laughed, then pulled her towards him again.

28

She looked so peaceful that he decided to let her sleep on.

Harry showered, dressed, then floated downstairs. He would make her breakfast. He was a happy, bouncy man.

He winked at Billy as he entered the kitchen. Billy, carrying a bowl of Rice Krispies overflowing in milk, scowled back and headed for the lounge. Harry lifted the milk carton from the counter and gave it a shake. Empty. *Thanks, Billy*. He threw it towards the pedal bin, but it bounced off the lid and landed a couple of feet away. Harry stepped over it to check the fridge. Then he pulled on his jacket and shouted to Billy that he was going to the garage for milk.

It was a beautiful spring morning. The air off the sea was fresh without being too cold and he walked quite happily the few hundred yards to the garage, his unbuttoned jacket flapping about him all the way. He remembered the last time he was at the garage . . .

I remember . . .

Harry stopped at the edge of the forecourt, his heart suddenly pumping hard.

What do I remember?

He looked at the petrol pumps, at the shop, at the serving hatch . . . *I was* . . . He heard voices, kids shouting, he had a sudden flash of lying on the damp, cold concrete and being . . .

A car honked behind him and Harry stepped quickly out of the way. A woman waved at him apologetically as she climbed out at one of the pumps. Harry waved back. He tried to remember what he'd been thinking about, but it was gone. He laughed. Probably something stupid.

He approached the serving hatch, but the kid behind pointed him towards the electronic doors. There was something vaguely familiar about the boy and he was smiling over like they were old friends. Probably a fan, Harry thought. *Prepare to sign an autograph*.

He walked down the aisle with a little wire basket in his hand. He got the milk, but then thought about making something extra special so that they could celebrate their happiness together. He picked up a pack of streaky bacon. Then some sausages. He added half a dozen eggs. He lifted a fry pack of potato bread, soda and pancake and held it to his nose. Ah, it smelled beautiful. It had been so long since he'd had a good fry-up. They could have a big family breakfast and look to the future.

He walked up to the counter, and the boy smiled at him. 'Are y'all right?' the boy asked.

'Fine, thanks.'

'Usual?'

Harry hesitated. Ah, now, that was it. He was a regular here, and the boy knew his habits. Fair enough. Harry nodded. The boy reached down a packet of cigarettes. Berkeley Menthol. The box was green, covered in cellophane. Harry ran his fingers over it. Had he smoked? Ruth had never mentioned it. He'd certainly enjoyed the odd puff when he was eighteen, but never when Ruth was around, she hadn't liked the smell. His parents had both smoked, but they'd forbidden him to. But when he was with his mates, sure, the odd one or two. He was sorely tempted. Sure he was a big boy now. Try it and see, he thought, if I don't like it, just throw them away.

'Anything else, sir?'

'Box of matches.'

Harry lit one up on the way home, pulling the collar of his jacket up to defeat the breeze.

Ah, now, wasn't that grand?

There was something about a cigarette. Something manly. He should have had one last night when he was all dolled up in the tux for Ruth. He would have looked like James Bond. *Have a sheat, Mish Moneypenny.* The cigarette, the tux, the soft-top TR7, his own live television show and a beautiful wife. It only remained to bring Billy round and he would have achieved a state of nirvana.

Billy was leaning against the door frame, idly running a toothbrush over his gums while Ruth stretched in bed.

She felt *marvellous*. Relaxed. Happy. Warm. 'Where's your father?'

'You mean the *stud*?' Billy drawled.

'Stop it.'

'He went to the garage. He might be back. I try not to keep track.' His mother's smile was telling him something he didn't want to know. But he had to ask. 'Are you still . . .?'

'Am I still what?'

'Getting divorced?'

Ruth looked suddenly gobsmacked. 'Shit! I was to phone her!'

With perfect timing a car horn sounded from outside: Ms Boyle, prepared to tear them asunder. Ruth jumped out of bed and started rummaging for something to pull on.

'Are you?' Billy asked.

'No!' She stopped and looked at him. 'Billy – don't make that face. Like it or not, he's your dad. He's getting better, we will make this work. Just give us a chance, eh? Be happy for us.'

'Yeah. Okay,' he said without conviction.

The horn sounded again.

'Shit! Billy, go out and tell her I've changed my mind. Tell her I'll call her!'

Billy shook his head, and said with a touch of glee: 'I think not. You've made your bed, and screwed in it.'

He pushed himself off the door.

'Billy!'

He was gone. 'Shit! Where're my shoes?!'

Ruth raced down the stairs a minute later, her feet working like pistons. She was wearing a T-shirt and a pair of black jeans. Her nose crinkled as she opened the front door. She tutted, and tried to remember the last time she'd eaten bacon. She'd already warned Billy once about eating fatty foods in front of his father, now she'd have to have another go at him.

She stepped outside.

Ms Boyle was leaning against the bonnet of her red BMW, arms folded, looking confident, composed, and in total, total control of her world. Her eyes flitted from Ruth's shoes to her jeans to her T-shirt, and she nodded approvingly. 'Casual, Ruth – but I like it.' Ruth, arms folded, approached cautiously and couldn't quite make herself look at her solicitor. It registered immediately.

'What's wrong?' Ms Boyle demanded abruptly.

Inside, Harry was halfway through production of the fry to end all fries. Eggs, bacon, black pudding, everything was bubbling away quite nicely. He had another cigarette as well. Half an inch of ash hung off it as he flipped his sausages.

The cordless phone rang on the counter beside him. He lifted it, then searched briefly for the answer button. A familiar voice sounded. JJ. Warning him not to turn up at court, that it would only make matters worse, if that were possible.

'Relax, JJ. I was just going to call you. The divorce is *off.'*

'Off?'

'We're staying married. It's all worked out well in the end.'

'Why, you wily old bugger. How'd you manage that?'

Outside, the colour had flamed onto Ms Boyle's

cheeks as Ruth defended her change of heart. 'That's all there is to it!' Ruth announced. 'I changed my mind!'

Boyle wagged a finger. Her nostrils flared. 'I don't understand you, Ruth! Years and years of misery and you just change your mind like that!'

'I know, but we're happy again! Now just go and tell them!' She turned on her heel, back towards the house.

'You are *not* happy!' Boyle shouted, then hurried after her.

'Yes, I am!'

'You *are not*!'

'What are you – on commission or something?'

Ruth went through the front door, and Boyle followed, still giving off.

Harry, meanwhile, had convinced JJ he really had managed to win Ruth over by fair means, and had moved on to his impending return to television. It was less than an hour away.

'Nervous?' he was saying. 'Yeah. I'm as nervous as hell. Live TV and I can't remember the half of it.'

Behind him the door opened. Ruth stopped dead, with her solicitor immediately behind.

'What is it they say, JJ?' Harry continued, unaware. 'You can fool some of the people some of the time . . . and here's me trying to fool all of the people all of the time . . .' He turned finally and saw Ruth. He smiled, the cigarette in his mouth finally dropping what was now an inch of ash onto the floor. Ruth watched as it landed on the milk carton that lay dripping several feet from the pedal bin. She took it all in, the stink of the sizzling food, the cigarette jammed in his mouth, the confession to JJ and finally the greasy, self-confident, pig invitation: 'Hiya,' he said, 'do you want a sausage?'

Ruth stepped sharply across the floor, and slapped the cigarette out of Harry's mouth. 'You bastard!' she cried.

Stunned, Harry took a step back. He spoke quickly into the phone – 'JJ, I have to go' – then set the phone back on the counter. He put a hand to his face. 'Jesus Christ, Ruth, what's the matter?'

'You are, you lying bastard! I gave you the benefit of the doubt!'

'What're you talking about? I was just telling JJ . . .'

'I heard what you were telling him!' She was completely enveloped by a cold white rage. She poked him in the chest. There was no holding back now. It all came pouring out. 'I made love to you because I so badly wanted to, because for a few days I've had the old you back, the old you I fell in love with . . . but now, this, *this* . . . smoking, this . . . *frying* . . .'

Harry stared incredulously at her. 'You're going to stop loving me over fags and food?'

'No, you fucking moron, because you lied to me! Because it's all been one big fucking act!'

'I just fancied a smoke! I didn't think . . .'

'That's just it! You never think!'

'Ruth, I'm sorry, I . . .' He came towards her, tried to take her in his arms, but she slapped him away.

'For twenty-five years you've done everything without bloody thinking! I don't know whether this has all been a big bloody charade or your memory's coming back . . . but I don't want it back! You may have forgotten the last twenty-five years, but I haven't, Harry.' Her sigh was like a death rattle. 'For fuck's sake, Harry, are you going to "not think" the next time some tart comes on to you? Or someone offers you a drink? Do you understand, Harry?' She raised her fist and pressed her knuckles, white and hard, against his brow. 'Do you have a conscience anywhere in there?'

She dropped her hand and looked despairingly at him.

'Ruth . . . *Ruth* . . .' Harry began softly, 'the last thing I want to do is hurt you . . .' He moved towards her again, but she backed away. 'Listen to me . . .'

'Leave me alone!' She spun on her heel and rushed out of the kitchen, leaving Ms Boyle standing smugly in the doorway.

She looked disdainfully at the shell-shocked Harry. 'Wanker,' she said, then followed her client.

Harry stood stunned for a moment, then the bitter smell of burning pork turned him back to the cooker. He swept the charred remains into the sink and turned on the water. He emerged from the cloud of steam at speed.

He passed Billy in the hallway. His son had his mobile phone clamped to his ear. A born reporter, already passing on the good news. 'Sister, darling, I think you might have been a little premature, or perhaps that was his problem. I'll keep you posted.'

He followed Harry out of the front door. Ruth was already sitting in Ms Boyle's car. Thankfully the solicitor, not to be rushed or intimidated, had taken her own haughty pace and Harry caught them just as she was starting the engine. He placed himself directly in front of the car.

'C'mon, Ruth, this is daft!'

Billy circled behind him, keeping up a running commentary. 'Face it, Harry, you threw it away! You dropped the baton on the final bend . . . you . . .'

'Will you fuck up?' Harry yelled.

'Oh and now the bad language as well. It's all falling apart, isn't it, Harry?'

Boyle leaned out of her window. 'Will you *please get out of the way*?'

'I'm not going anywhere.'

'Drive over him,' Ruth instructed.

'I'll have you arrested!' Boyle threatened.

'I want to speak to my wife.'

From behind, Billy said: 'Actions speak louder than words, fat boy.'

Ruth put her hand on the steering wheel. 'Okay, just for a minute.'

'*Ruth . . .*'

'Please.'

Boyle rolled her eyes, then reduced the revs. Ruth rolled down her window. Harry cautiously moved from the front along to the passenger door. Out of the side of her mouth Ruth said, 'Now, drive!'

'What? Oh . . . !'

Boyle's foot hit the pedal and the car vaulted forward, spewing up dirt and weeds and leaving Harry standing helpless amidst a cloud of dust.

'Ruth!' he called after her, but she was gone.

'*Sucker.*' Billy said gleefully from the doorway.

Harry glanced back at him, then returned his gaze to the rapidly disappearing vehicle.

Billy was searching for something suitably withering to say when his father suddenly dropped down onto his arse in the drive.

Billy straightened, suddenly panicked. *He hasn't gone and had a friggin' heart attack . . .*

He cautiously approached.

Harry's shoulders began to pump up and down, his head held low between them.

Was he laughing?

Billy ventured slowly round, trying to get a better look.

Christ, he's blubbering like a baby.

He'd never seen anything like it. His dad's whole body was shaking. Tears were flooding out of his eyes, even his nose and mouth seemed to be leaking. He was absolutely devastated.

Billy didn't know what to do.

They had defeated his father. But this wasn't what he had expected. He'd thought the mask might fall now that he'd been exposed. That his father's performance over the past few weeks would finally get cancelled and he'd admit defeat with a wry smile or a flurry of curses, emerging once again as the brigand of old. They had fought a lengthy duel. He was Robin Hood and his dad was the Sheriff of Nottingham, Captain Hook, Boo Radley and Gary Glitter rolled into one.

But here he was, falling to pieces before his very eyes.

This wasn't just another Harry McKee backfire. It was . . .

Jesus, what if he really . . .

Billy knelt down beside his father. Hesitantly he placed a hand on his shoulder. Harry turned away, wiping the sleeve of his shirt across his face. Okay, Billy thought, a little gentle sparring, let's see what he's made of.

'I heard you making love to Mum last night,' Billy said. It sat in the sea air for several moments. Jab again, harder. 'Did she have an orgasm?'

'God Almighty,' Harry said.

Left hook. 'I was wondering if women here lie back and think of England, or the occupied six counties?'

Harry shook his head, then wiped at his tears again. 'You should write my scripts,' he said, then climbed laboriously back to his feet. He paused for a moment, then bent down and kissed Billy on the top of the head.

Billy didn't know what to do, say, how to react. He was momentarily struck dumb.

Harry turned and walked back around the side of the house towards the car. He felt in his pocket for the keys, then opened it up and climbed in behind the wheel.

'Are you going to court?' Billy asked, quickly coming up to the window.

'What's the point? She's made up her mind.'

His father started the engine. The despair was

sitting thick on his father's face. Billy had a sudden vision of his father gassing himself in the car, or driving off the pier, some form of suicide. 'Where are you going, then?'

'Where do you think?' said Harry. 'While she's in court divorcing me I'll be cooking lunch for half a million people.'

Harry moved the car slowly forward. 'See you,' he said.

'Dad . . .' Billy began, but Harry just shook his head and drove on.

Billy watched as the car pulled out onto the main road and turned towards Belfast.

He sighed. He understood that growing up was difficult, but nobody had warned him that it would be this bloody difficult.

Everything he had planned, everything he had schemed for, everything he had dreamed of, fantasized about, it had all just been handed to him on a plate.

Then he had seen his father in pieces in the dirt, and the plate was suddenly made of paper and damp with tears.

'Fuck it!' Billy shouted to nobody, and everybody.

Then he started to run.

29

JJ found Ruth and Ms Boyle leaning against a car parked on double yellow lines outside Belfast Magistrates' Court. Ruth was smoking. This was NOT A GOOD SIGN.

He was well aware that he was not adept at showing understanding, or offering sympathy or advice. He was a solicitor, and should have been skilled at all three, but it was just the way of him. He would tell an agoraphobic to get out and enjoy himself. A depressive to cheer up. And a best friend, whose memory was beginning to return, but whose wife had left him and was demanding an instant divorce? What could he do but mumble down the phone, mouthing witless platitudes and only just stop short of offering a number for the Samaritans. He left Harry with a promise that he would do his best to talk Ruth out of this rash turnaround, which in itself followed another rash turnaround . . . maybe they could use that, maybe it showed that she was the one who was unbalanced, maybe . . .

'No,' Harry said, 'it's over.'

'Harry . . .'

'Over.'

He thought Harry was surprisingly calm. Too calm. 'Where are you now, Harry?' JJ asked.

'Queen Elizabeth Bridge.'

'You're not thinking of doing anything silly, are you, Harry?'

'Yes, I am. Cooking breakfast for half the nation.'

'You're going ahead . . .'

'Yes.'

'You're sure that's wise?'

'No.'

'Okay, Harry, have it your way. I'll do my best at this end.'

But, as ever, his best was barely adequate. He rushed up to her, all breathless, papers spilling out of his files. 'Ruth, I . . .'

'Don't,' Ruth said flatly, looking straight ahead.

'Bugger off,' said Ms Boyle.

'He really tried, Ruth. Don't do this. It'll destroy him.'

'Don't listen to him,' said Boyle, 'you're doing the right thing.'

JJ stood directly in front of Ruth, trying to do the eye-to-eye solicitor thing, but she looked straight through him. 'He's poured his whole heart out to me, Ruth. I've never seen a man so torn apart. He loves you. You know he does.'

'Well, maybe love isn't enough.'

It was stark, it was final.

'Well, can he at least keep the car?'

Ruth tutted and pushed herself off the car. She threw the half-smoked cigarette to the ground and stamped on it. 'C'mon,' she said to Boyle, and they both strode off up the steps and into the court building.

JJ remained outside, pacing up and down. There was a pub much favoured by the legal profession just across the road and round the corner, maybe a quick . . .

'Where are they?'

He turned, he squinted against the morning sun. . A teenager, short dark hair, more than a passing resemblance to . . .

'I *said* where are they?'

'Billy? Why, haven't you grown into the big fella! Last time I saw you . . .'

'Will you quit your fuckin' slabbering and tell me where they are?'

JJ's mouth dropped open, then he pointed vaguely towards the court. 'They . . . they're in . . . ah . . . come with me.'

He led Billy up the stairs and along the corridor to what was known as the Angry Room where married couples about to be divorced waited for their cases to be called to court. There was no actual rule about where people sat, but the women would always be found on one side and the men on the other. Children sometimes played in between. In JJ's time he'd seen any number of fist fights, three reconciliations and one birth in this room, but today it was quiet. Three women and their solicitors on one side, a solitary man on the other. Billy rushed up to his mother.

'Billy . . .?' Ruth said, surprised. 'Where's your father? Is he . . .?' Billy shook his head. 'What're you doing here?'

'I . . . are we sure we want to do this?'

'Billy?'

There was an usher in the doorway. 'McKee versus McKee!'

'That's us,' said Ms Boyle.

Just over a mile away, Harry slowed his car to a halt. He was about three hundred yards from the security gates. There was a crowd gathered outside them.

Ronnie was strutting about, trying to keep them orderly.

Harry checked himself in the mirror.

That face. That *old* face. He shook his head. He was used to it now. It didn't seem that old. He stroked the smooth skin where he'd shaved. He checked his eyes, they were only slightly red despite his tears. He felt no more like doing this live television than flying to the moon. But he had to. He had to discover if he could do it, if it was in him. He was aware that things were starting to come back to him. Even on the drive over there had been flashes, just little things, little incidents. But there was still so much more to learn about himself.

Last night he'd made love to a beautiful woman, a woman who loved him.

Nobody could change that.

He put the car back into gear and rolled slowly up to the gates. He was spotted immediately. Old women, old men pressed forward. Harry rolled the window down.

'Harry! We're so pleased you're back!'

'That other guy's a waste of space! Welcome back, Harry!'

Harry smiled, he shook hands, it was nice. 'Thank you . . . thank you . . . good to be back . . . hope you enjoy the show . . .'

Ronnie elbowed his way through and asked to see his security clearance. Harry handed him his pass. Ronnie studied it, then studied Harry, then turned his attention back to the card. 'Everything seems to be in order, Mr Magee,' he said, handing it back.

'Thanks very much,' said Harry.

The gate was raised, and Harry drove on through to the car park while Ronnie manhandled some pensioners out of his way.

There were flowers in his dressing room. Dozens of cards. He drummed his fingers nervously on the arm of his chair as Lily finished his make-up.

'You'll be fine, Harry,' Lily said. 'Is Ruth watching?'

'Who, my ex-wife?'

Lily rolled her eyes. 'Och, Harry, not again.'

Harry shrugged. 'Still,' he said, 'at least I'm not drinking.' Then he hiccuped. 'Joke,' he added, just in case.

'I thought youse might have sorted it out.'

'So did I.'

Frankie Woods arrived, all smiles. 'All set, Harry?'

'All set.'

'You're gonna kill 'em.'

'Every last one.'

'Where's that gorgeous wife of yours?' Frankie boomed. 'That rock of Gibraltar? That vision without whom we wouldn't have you here today? She should be here. You should interview her.'

'Busy.' Harry said. 'But good idea.'

'Another time, okay?' Harry nodded. Frankie rubbed his hands together. 'Okay, champ, let's get this show on the road.'

Harry winked at Lily, then got up out of his chair. He had a script in his lap, but he knew it off by heart.

Frankie led him through to the studio floor. The sound man attached a radio mike and earpiece while Harry stared at the set. He'd rehearsed here constantly during the past week, but this was different. There was a clock counting down. There was an audience whispering excitedly. There were television commercials playing on a dozen monitors. Harry hopped from foot to foot.

'Nervous?' said the sound man.

Harry nodded.

'Nothing to be nervous about,' said Frankie, 'you'll fly through it. But not too fast, mind. Take your time.' He put his arm around him and squeezed. 'You'll be great. I'll look after you.' Harry nodded. Frankie hurried off to the gallery.

Lily retouched his make-up. 'You're sweating,' she said. Harry nodded. This *was* different. Hundreds of thousands of people. *I'm getting divorced*. All waiting to see him fall flat on his face. *Even now she's throwing her wedding ring in the sea.* He had a sudden urge to run away and hide. *My wife despises me, my son hates me, I'm trying to cook eggs and I'll have no house, no home, and as soon as I bugger this up I'll have no job. I'll be sleeping on the beach.*

The floor manager was smiling beside him. The theme tune to *What's Cookin'?* began to blast out across the studio. Harry's shirt stuck instantly to his back. A voice boomed over the PA: 'AND NOW LIVE FROM BELFAST, IT'S THE BIG MAC HIMSELF, HE'S BACK IN BUSINESS . . . IT'S HARRY McKEE!'

Run! Run away! Now!

The audience rose to their feet. 'Ha-rry! Ha-rry! Harry!'

There was a Mexican wave.

The floor manager gave him a shove in the back, propelling him out under the lights and into the cheers and adulation. He skipped across the floor. The assistant floor manager threw a tea towel towards him, as rehearsed, and he caught it first time and tossed it lazily around his shoulders like a scarf, before coming to a halt on his mark, a dozen feet short of the autocue and only a little further from the audience.

Across the Province, in houses, in homes, the old, the unemployed, the disabled, the single mothers, the mothers, the curious, the confused, they all sat to watch the return of Harry McKee. Claire was at home in her apartment, tingling with excitement. 'C'mon, Daddy,' she told the screen, 'knock 'em dead!'

'Fade music . . . milk the applause,' Frankie directed, up in the gallery. He twitched nervously. Harry had a face on him like a death mask. 'Are you happy, Harry?' Frankie asked. There was a slight nod. 'Then tell your face.'

There was no perceptible change in Harry's demeanour. The signature tune was almost gone. The audience settled down. Harry stood staring at them.

'It's all yours, kid,' said Frankie.

Harry continued to stare.

'*C'mon*, Harry,' said Frankie.

Harry was thinking of Ruth and how he'd lost her. Of Billy. Of Claire. *Looking gormless*. And here he was looking gormless in front of half the nation. Yet he couldn't move.

Beside Frankie, his assistant said, 'Five seconds in, he's five seconds over.'

The audience was starting to fidget with embarrassment.

'C'mon, Harry,' said Frankie again. He could feel the blood draining from his face.

'C'mon, Daddy,' Claire said to his frozen features.

She was right to divorce him for what he'd done over the years. She was right not to trust him. He had been so close to winning her back. In fact – he *had* won her back. Just for a few glorious hours, but it was over.

Should he try again? Even if he met with some success, wouldn't he ultimately just be putting her through all that misery once more?

He should give her her freedom.

Wasn't it more important that she be happy? If that was what it took, then yes, let her go. Let her make her own life.

Frankie's assistant whispered: 'Will I cut . . .'

But Frankie's eyes had narrowed, he raised his palm to stop her. On screen, slowly, slowly, a smile was starting to meander across Harry's face, then there was a hint of a twinkle in his eyes . . .

'Well, that got your attention,' Harry said suddenly, and the audience erupted.

Then he was down amongst them, shaking hands, smiling, waving. Claire hugged herself. Frankie rolled his eyes and blew air out of his puffed-up cheeks.

'It's been a long time,' Harry told the audience, told the country, 'and it's good to be back. Thanks for all the cards, and I'll get round to replying once I can afford the stamps . . .' They laughed. 'In case you

don't know I'm getting divorced today.' *AWWWWWWW.*
'So if any of you have a spare room . . .?' Half a dozen
wrinkled hands shot up.

'Back on track, Harry, please,' Frankie said.

Harry stepped back out of the audience and looked
immediately to the autocue. 'On today's show, banish
those vampires with new adventures in garlic . . .
the books you'll be reading in Benidorm this summer,
and in part two . . . Liam Neeson!' The audience
broke into applause. He milked it for a few moments,
then added. 'His stunt double tells us what it's like
to get all of the bruises and none of the acclaim.'
They groaned – but they loved it.

He was enjoying this.

It was easy.

He felt a warmth, he felt love, he felt in control,
more than he had done at any single moment since
he'd been in hospital.

How many men could stand like this in front of
thousands of people and feel so totally relaxed?

He launched into the first item.

'How're we doing?' Frankie asked.

'We're doing okay,' said his assistant.

'Garlic makes us think of vampires and Frenchmen,
and sure, what's the difference . . .' He was chopping
away. The audience was lapping it up. Happy. Secure.
'Just watch the tips of those fingers . . . like myself,

garlic has had something of a bad press over the years . . .'

'BASTARD!'

Frankie sat suddenly bolt upright. He studied the monitors. Someone in the audience . . .

'See what I mean?' Harry laughed and the audience laughed with him. They looked around them, wondering what the joke was, wondering what Harry had set up for them now. He'd done that before, planting a comedian in amongst them, winding them up. 'But really,' Harry continued, 'sometimes it's hard to . . .'

'YOU COMPLETE BASTARD!'

Harry gazed into the audience. The studio lights didn't make it very easy to see. This time there was a slightly more anxious buzz about them, but Harry felt fine. He was flush with adrenaline. It was like a drug. The secret was controlling it, not letting it control you. That's where he'd gone wrong in the past. But now, now he was on top, he was at peace, he was . . .

'BASTARD BASTARD BASTARD!'

Frankie had her. Three rows from the back. Woman, red outfit, long hair. 'Ignore it, Harry,' he urged. 'We'll get her out.'

He was pressing the buzzer for security, but when he glanced at the exterior monitor he saw that

Ronnie was lying underneath a post van, checking for bombs.

'Ah now,' Harry said, 'the beauty of live television.' He smiled winningly. He had been watching a lot of television and knew that these days producers loved playing tricks on their presenters. It made for good TV. Good ratings. Just play along. Still, it was a bit rich doing it on his first day back. Maybe it was a test, to see if he was really back on form. Handle this, he could handle anything. 'If you've something to say, madam, why don't you come down here and say it?'

The audience broke into applause. That was it, call Frankie's bluff.

'*Harry!*' Frankie said.

The woman was up out of her seat and coming somewhat awkwardly down the steps onto the studio floor.

'It's okay,' Harry told the audience, flourishing the knife he'd been chopping the garlic with, 'I'm armed.' They laughed weakly. The woman came to a halt a few yards short of him. She blinked at the sudden intensity of the lights, she glanced about her, suddenly not quite as confident. 'Now, madam, what seems to be the problem?'

The audience was wondering who the comedienne was, and what her punch line would be.

Her punch line was to remove a gun from her bag and point it at Harry.

There was a communal *ohhhhh!* from the audience, and in homes across the country. Claire's heart stopped. Then started. In the gallery Frankie uttered a stunned, 'Ho-ly ffuck! Call the police! Call them *now.*'

'Cut transmission?'

'Are you joking! I've waited twenty years for something like this. You'll cut over my dead body.'

'Or Harry's,' his assistant said, although under her breath.

Harry eyed the gun with only a slight hint of nervousness. He was pretty sure a flag would come out of it with *Bang* written on it. Or it would be made of chocolate and the mad woman would take a bite out of it.

And yet, the gun was shaking.

The woman was sweating.

Slowly she raised her free hand as if to scratch her head, then suddenly pulled at her hair and it all came away. A wig fell to the floor.

Harry felt a slap to his face, but it wasn't real it was . . .

The past.

The breakdown.

His final, embarrassing show.

The same dress the woman had worn and yet . . . and yet this was a man. With make-up, mascara . . .

'Walter . . .?' Harry ventured. 'Walter *Adair*?'

His name fizzed around the audience. Walter Adair? *The* Walter Adair?

The misshapen carrot. Firm young bodies. His wife storming off . . .

Harry was suddenly unsure. What was Frankie thinking of, bringing Walter back like this?

Okay, keep calm, live TV, play along, it's a great laugh, sink or swim . . .

'That really suits you,' Harry said.

'Don't start!' Walter hissed, brandishing the gun. His voice was ragged, his eyes red and moist. 'Because of you I lost my job, my wife left me and I tried to commit suicide.'

His lines weren't the funniest, but maybe they were building to something. Play along. Keep it light. Maybe *gunge* would fall from the ceiling. 'Yeah . . .' Harry said, searching desperately for a line, 'yeah . . . but, honest to God, Walter, you look great in that . . .'

Walter pulled the trigger. There was a loud *crack!* and the knife Harry had all but forgotten shot out of his hand, taking a sliver of flesh with it. There were screams from the audience. Harry stumbled back, bleeding.

Wild About Harry

Holy Christ, Holy Christ, Holy Christ, Holy Christ . . . !
No joke, no joke, no joke, no joke . . .

He was backed up against the counter. He held on to it with one hand and clutched the other against his thumping chest.

This is a nightmare. Wake up! Wake up! It's happening again!

Walter was right beside him. 'You ruined me! You destroyed my life!'

'Walter . . .'

'Everything I had, everything I dreamed of, all gone because of you.'

'Walter . . .'

'Shut up! You destroyed my world, for nothing, for no reason other than because you felt like it!'

Harry was staring into the abyss.

He was expecting to die. He couldn't get his breath, he was dizzy, he felt light . . .

No. Stop it. Don't fall.

This *is* happening. Deal with it.

Walter was right.

He had destroyed him. As he had destroyed everything that was dear to him. His wife. His son. His daughter only tolerated him because she didn't live with him. It seemed to be his only talent in life: destruction.

What sort of a life was that?

A sudden and surprising feeling of calm washed over him. His head cleared; he was aware of the blood, but unaware of the pain. He blinked into Walter's dark, hollowed face.

'Walter,' he said quietly, 'I'm really sorry. But I wasn't well that day. Any other time I couldn't have given a rat's arse about your love life. You were just in the wrong place at the wrong time.'

Upstairs, Frankie's assistant said, 'Network's on line, they want to go live over the UK.'

Frankie nodded, then whispered into Harry's earpiece. 'Harry, you finally got network. Hold it together. Help's on its way.'

He didn't want help. He slipped the earpiece out. Walter was right. His life wasn't worth living.

Cooking on TV? Who was he kidding?

He was a joke. A national disgrace. A personal nightmare.

Frankie had probably engineered this to get revenge.

Or Ruth.

Walter's teeth were black with neglect. There was spittle flying out of his mouth as he yelled in Harry's ear.

'I don't want to hear your pathetic little excuses! I died on live television, and now so will you!'

He pressed the barrel hard against Harry's temple.

'Say goodbye, Harry,' Walter whispered. There was a smile of triumph. His finger curled around the trigger and began to squeeze.

Harry smiled. 'Aw, fuck it, Walter, go ahead, if it makes you happy.'

'What?' He hadn't expected *this*. He had expected more begging. Tears. He wanted to humiliate him, reduce him to *nothing*, let him know how it felt, and then kill him.

'Pull the trigger, make my day.'

'Wh-what are you talking about?'

'We've both been living a double life, haven't we?'

'Shut up!' Walter pressed the barrel with renewed vigour into Harry's brow.

Harry pressed his head back against it with just as much strength, shook his head against it. 'Go on, do it, do it, do it now.'

'You really want me to?'

'Yes, yes! Do it, come on, Walter – do it. I want you to.'

'But *why*?'

'Because we're the same! Our little secrets, Walter. Public you, private you. Private me, public me.'

Walter glanced around, checking for company, but the whole world seemed frozen. Secure in that knowledge, he moved the gun back a fraction. 'You can't talk your way out of this!' he hissed.

'I don't intend to, Walter. I *want* you to shoot me.'

'Why?'

'Because up until two weeks ago I existed only on videotape and in other people's bad memories. I didn't know what was going on! I was an innocent for about six seconds and then all of this crap started to catch up with me and I couldn't understand it . . . and then I found out what I was and it frightened me to death. I've been trying to make amends ever since, but it's just not working! You can't go back, you can't undo the mistakes. Walter, you know that as much as I do . . .'

'Will you shut up, *now*?'

Harry hesitated for a moment. Then slowly he shook his head. There were *ooohs* from the audience. No, if he was going to die, then he was going to say it and be done. He had nothing to fear, because he had nothing to lose. He had lost it already.

'Walter, I *understand*. I lost my wife too, and I wronged her, just as you did . . .'

'I didn't . . .'

'Shut up and listen.' The gun flexed upwards again, but he didn't shoot. 'My wife loved me to bits,' said Harry, 'but in return I destroyed her life. It took me a while, but I managed it. Then I was given a second chance.' He sighed. 'Do you know where I should be now? Standing in a court trying to persuade her to stick with me for another twenty-five miserable years. But I'm not, because even though it breaks my heart, deep down I know that's what she truly deserves. A new life. So if you think it's important, fire away, Walter; make my day.'

Walter thought for a moment, thought about the loneliness and the nightmares and the terror and the fact that *everything* had gone down the plughole. And that this excuse for a man was the reason for it all.

'Okay,' he said.

He raised the gun for the final time.

'Just one minute!'

A woman's voice, a figure moving towards him out of the lights. Walter turned, aimed. 'Get the fuck out of it!'

Ruth stepped onto the set of *What's Cookin'?* 'I can't,' she said, 'not after that speech.'

Walter followed her with his gun as she crossed the set. 'I'm warning you . . .'

She ignored him. She was standing over Harry. 'Did you write that in advance or is it straight off the top of your head?'

'Top of my head,' said Harry, 'though it's a big head.'

Walter brandished the gun at Ruth's face. 'I swear to God . . .' he began, but she stopped him dead with a snapped: 'Just give us a minute, for God's sake!'

Then she turned her attention back to Harry.

Walter was struck momentarily impotent.

'I thought you were in court,' Harry said.

'I was.'

'You mean you changed your mind?'

'No, Harry. We're divorced. I have the house. Most of your income. And the judge is going to throw you in jail if you come within half a mile of me again. It's pretty much your worst nightmare.'

Harry shook his head. 'Losing you is my worst nightmare.'

'Sweet, but it won't . . .'

Walter was suddenly in between them, spitting out: 'Do you mind? I'm trying to kill him!'

Ruth's brow furrowed. 'Do I mind? For God's sake, man, I'm trying to say something important here and it isn't easy!'

Walter looked incredulously at her. He waved the gun in her face again. 'What are you, some sort of lunatic? I've got a *gun*!'

'And I've . . .'

She suddenly snapped her knee upwards, smacking it perfectly into his groin. Walter's finger squeezed the trigger reflexively as the blow struck home and a gunshot brought screams of terror from the audience, but it only blew a hole in the scenery somewhere off behind Ruth. Walter's mouth opened and closed rapidly as he gasped for air, then he slowly collapsed to his knees. Then he rolled over and lay in a heap, groaning on the floor of the studio. The audience sat stunned as two armed police officers jumped onto the set and immediately pinned Walter to the floor.

The audience clapped with relief, then stopped as soon as it became clear that the drama wasn't quite over.

Ruth had swatted Walter like a fly, and now she was looming over Harry. The audience sat mesmerized, not just in the studio, but in homes across the country. Reporters who'd been giving a running commentary fell silent as Ruth placed a hand on the counter on either side of her ex-husband. Her voice was taut, determined. He stared into her eyes. There was only Ruth and Harry, oblivious of a watching world.

'Now you just listen to me,' Ruth said sternly.

Half the fucking country was listening to her.

Half the world, for all Frankie knew.

'You *did* get a second chance,' Ruth said, 'and you did fuck it up, but maybe I did as well. Maybe I tried to make you something you never were, never could be. But I do know one thing, I still love you, and if we're going to make a go of this we have to take it one tiny step at a time.'

She reached into her pocket and removed her wedding ring. She set it down on the counter beside him.

'We're divorced, Harry McKee,' she said bluntly. 'You move out, you get yourself an apartment, you think about what you want to do with your life, who you want to go to the movies with, who you want to eat lunch with, who you want to make love to. If you decide it's me, then you get rid of all the other crap in your life, you phone me up and you ask me out on a date. And if I'm not doing anything more interesting, we'll take it from there, okay?'

He gazed at her, amazed. Reborn. Rejuvenated. Re-everything. 'Okay.'

'Okay.'

She turned and began to walk away.

'Ruth?'

'What?'

'I love you too.'

She stopped, she shook her head, and then she ran back into his arms and they kissed.

The studio audience rose to its feet and cheered. They began to chant, *'Harry! Harry! Harry!'* Upstairs, Frankie wiped a tear from his eye. At home, Claire pressed tissues to her face to try and stem the flow. All over the friggin' place people were crying at the happiness of it all.

Finally Ruth broke off, she glanced shyly at the audience, then hurried away across the set.

'Ruth!'

She stopped again. 'What, Harry?'

'I'll call you tonight.'

'No! Jesus, Harry! Don't you listen, I said . . .'

But she was drowned out in the sweep of the theme music to *What's Cookin?* Harry turned perfectly to camera. He didn't even need the autocue. 'On tomorrow's show we'll be on the Orient Express, that's chicken chow mein in twenty minutes. Plus Leo Sayer, whatever happened to him?' He raised his bloody hand to the audience. 'Don't go away now!' he bellowed. They were on their feet again and cheering.

Harry whipped off his tea towel, threw it to the assistant floor manager, pointed at the monitor and said, 'Roll titles!'

Then he went after Ruth.

Epilogue

Their second marriage was postponed exactly three hours and fourteen minutes before the ceremony was due to take place.

They thought the hospital was a much better place for their daughter, Rose, five pounds, three ounces and three weeks premature, to be born rather than the registry office.

A month later, they reconvened, and were remarried. JJ was best man. Billy would have been, but there was a massive blow-up over a hair cut and he was relegated by mutual agreement to usher. He still made a speech. He still doesn't get on that well with his father, and vice versa, but they're getting there.

Against custom, the bride wore white. For a joke JJ switched the tapes just as Ruth came down the aisle. 'Shotgun Wedding' rang out, and she didn't see the funny side of it.

But she's happy, most of the time.

Harry doesn't drink, much, and when he parties, she is always with him. He doesn't smoke, often, but when he does he makes sure his wife has one as well.

He hasn't looked at another woman, and doesn't care to.

He lived in his own apartment for three weeks before moving home to their house in Donaghadee. The first thing she made him do was paint over Aladdin Sane, and she was just in time to stop him replacing it with a mural featuring Gary Glitter. She had to explain the significance of that one, and also why he shouldn't sing 'Do You Want to Touch!' when he went to the swimming pool.

Harry was offered the chance to go to London to present his own chat show. He turned it down.

Instead *What's Cookin'?* is broadcast across the United Kingdom on Channel 4 in the mornings, although there is a time delay in case there are any 'mishaps'. *What's Cookin'?* has also been sold into syndication and appears on more than sixty-three television stations around the world.

Harry sometimes gets fan mail from Croatia.
He always replies.
He can afford the stamps.

Author's Note

Five years ago, when I was still working on the *County Down Spectator*, one of my colleagues, Karen Patterson, passed a clipping from a newspaper to me and said, here, that sounds like the sort of thing you could make a story out of.

Now the bane of any writer's life is *anyone* who says, *you could write a story about that*. Generally these suggestions are the *last* thing you could imagine writing something about. Generally you want to get out a big stick and beat the living daylights out of anyone who suggests *you could write a story about that*.

But on this occasion Karen had unwittingly stumbled upon something that would ultimately change the face of modern literature. Unfortunately she kept that for herself, but the clipping she passed to me certainly looked interesting enough for me to file away in my Must-Think-About drawer: it was a two- or three-paragraph news report about a man in England who'd been in an accident and suddenly couldn't remember anything after the age of eighteen, couldn't remember his wife, his job, basically anything about his adult life.

Coincidentally, that very afternoon, the good people at BBC Northern Ireland phoned. They had at this stage taken an option on my first novel *Divorcing Jack* and knew I was keen to get involved in writing screenplays – did I, they wondered, have any ideas that might lend themselves to a feature film?

Did I 'eck as like! (I was going through my *Coronation Street* phase at the time.)

As it happens, chuck, I responded, I've just had this idea about someone who loses his memory and has to rebuild and rediscover his life.

And thus was born *Wild About Harry*, the screenplay (and, Karen, there's a book token on its way to you even as I write this; you can't say I'm not generous).

So why a novel as well?

With any film there is a huge amount of writing that goes on that never makes it as far as the screen, and *Wild About Harry* is no exception. A ninety-minute film is by necessity pretty lean and mean when it comes to detail, and that is right and proper, but it also meant that I was left knowing so much about the characters. Without getting too pretentious about it – oh, all right, why shouldn't I? – I'd lived with them for years, organized their love lives, changed their jobs, decided what clothes they wore, what songs they listened to. I knew them better than I knew myself – well, my next-door neighbour at least. I thought it would be a terrible waste to just discard it all or bore people at parties with their back story. So I wrote this. It is, in effect, *The Screenwriter's Cut*.

Screenwriting, after the first draft, is always a team game, and in that respect both Robert Cooper, the producer, and the film's director, Declan Lowney, made huge contributions to the finished script, and therefore also to the novel, although obviously not enough to entitle them to royalties. Laurie Borg, Nik Powell, David Thompson, Kate Triggs, Kate Croft, a small lady who made the tea, a mouse called Eric, and the African Children's Choir also all made helpful suggestions. If I've forgotten anyone, well, blame Harry.

COLIN BATEMAN
April 2000

Belfast Confidential

Bateman

They say moving house is one of the most stressful things you can do. Well, as far as Dan Starkey's concerned, 'they' can stick it because right now unpacking is the least of his worries . . .

No sooner has Dan moved house, than his best mate, Mouse, is brutally murdered – leaving him to catch a killer, become Editor of scandal magazine *Belfast Confidential*, and compile its much-coveted Power List edition.

But he's not the only one with a hit list to complete. Someone's systematically killing local celebrities and unless Dan can stop them the magazine's going under and so is he . . . by about six feet.

Yep ñ from where Dan's standing, lugging furniture about looks pretty damn tempting.

IF YOU HAVEN'T READ A BATEMAN NOVEL BEFORE, THIS IS WHAT YOU'RE MISSING:

'As sharp as a pint of snakebite' *The Sunday Times*

'Witty, fast-paced and throbbing with menace' *Time Out*

'If Roddy Doyle was as good as people say, he would probably write novels like this' *Arena*

978 0 7553 0927 6

headline

Chapter and Verse

Colin Bateman

Writer Ivan Connor is desperate. His publisher has turned down his wonderful new novel, his agent is out of ideas, and the only person to turn up at his latest reading is his mum. He's deeply jealous of the marketable Francesca Brady, a hugely successful author of fat romantic books for fat romantic people, whose expansive hair and bright red lipstick mock him from posters everywhere he goes. He's also living at home since his marriage broke up, and he's just collected the wrong child from school.

But one night Connor stumbles on a route back to the top, via a beautiful model, two deranged psychopaths, a multi-million-pound publishing fraud, true love and utter heartbreak . . .

IF YOU HAVEN'T READ A COLIN BATEMAN NOVEL BEFORE, THIS IS WHAT YOU'RE MISSING

'A joy from start to finish . . . witty, fast-paced and throbbing with menace' *Time Out*

'As sharp as a pint of snakebite' *Sunday Times*

'There is more to Bateman than a racy plot. His prose is intelligent as well as aesthetically satisfying, his dialogue toughly funny and tone-perfect' *Mail on Sunday*

978 0 7553 0246 8

headline

I Predict A Riot

Bateman

Superintendent James 'Marsh' Mallow, of Belfast CID, wants just one thing before he retires – to pin something on the notorious Pink Harrison. And when a dismembered body turns up, Mallow's convinced he's finally got his man. Problem is, take Pink down and trouble of the full-scale rioting kind is likely to flare up.

Mallow's prepared to risk it but he's not counted on a litigious lady of the night, a civil servant who's infatuated with a carrot-cake-induced coma victim, 'Steve' in 'Office 12' or terrorist and occasional birdwatcher, Redmond.

In a city where everyone's got something on somebody else (except for 'Steve' who's got *everything* on *everybody*), it's only a matter of time before things really kick off . . .

Bateman: the word on the street:

'Sometimes brutal, often blackly humorous and always terrific' *Observer*

'He delivers an extraordinary mix of plots and characters . . . colourful, zany, absurd and surreal' *The Times*

'Bateman writes with sympathy and humour' *Daily Telegraph*

978 0 7553 3467 4

headline